A DIVIDED INHERITANCE

When Amanda is summoned home to help her father and step-mother, Kelly, by looking after her young half-brothers and sister whilst the couple go away on holiday, she doesn't realise that a family tragedy isn't far away. And what complicates matters is the presence of Kelly's younger brother, Simon — who then demands his rights to a share of what could turn out to be a divided inheritance.

SPECIAL MESSAGE TO READERS

This book is published under the auspices of

THE ULVERSCROFT FOUNDATION

(registered charity No. 264873 UK)

Established in 1972 to provide funds for research, diagnosis and treatment of eye diseases. Examples of contributions made are: —

A Children's Assessment Unit at Moorfield's Hospital, London.

•

Twin operating theatres at the Western Ophthalmic Hospital, London.

•

A Chair of Ophthalmology at the Royal Australian College of Ophthalmologists.

•

The Ulverscroft Children's Eye Unit at the Great Ormond Street Hospital For Sick Children, London.

You can help further the work of the Foundation by making a donation or leaving a legacy. Every contribution, no matter how small, is received with gratitude. Please write for details to:

THE ULVERSCROFT FOUNDATION,
The Green, Bradgate Road, Anstey,
Leicester LE7 7FU, England.
Telephone: (0116) 236 4325

In Australia write to:

THE ULVERSCROFT FOUNDATION,
c/o The Royal Australian and New Zealand College of Ophthalmologists,
94-98 Chalmers Street, Surry Hills,
N.S.W. 2010, Australia

KAREN ABBOTT

A DIVIDED INHERITANCE

Complete and Unabridged

LINFORD
Leicester

First published in Great Britain in 20[illegible]08

First Linford Edition
published [illegible]

British Library CIP Data

Abbott, Karen
A divided inheritance.—Large print ed.—
Linford romance library
1. Love stories
2. Large type books
I. Title
823.9′2 [F]

ISBN 978–1–84782–602–2

Published by
F. A. Thorpe (Publishing)
Anstey, Leicestershire

Set by Words & Graphics Ltd.
Anstey, Leicestershire
Printed and bound in Great Britain by
T. J. International Ltd., Padstow, Cornwall

This book is printed on acid-free paper

1

Amanda Purvey sank on to the sofa with a sigh of relief, thankful that no-one from the hotel where she and her flat-mates worked could see her. Cucumber gel face packs were not for general viewing! She planned to read the next few chapters of a heart-warming saga set in the Lake District by one of her favourite authors whilst the face-pack performed its promised wonders.

In the midst of a tender moment between the feisty heroine and the devastatingly handsome hero the telephone shrilled. Amanda reluctantly laid down her book and went to pick up the phone, just knowing it would be someone wanting one of the other girls.

She was wrong.

'Is that you, Amanda?'

Amanda's heart sank, her expression

involuntarily changed into a wry grimace. It was Kelly, her father's second wife. They had never got on well together . . . too similar in age, Amanda supposed. Kelly, an aspiring model, had only been twenty-three when she and her dad were married.

Amanda couldn't remember when Kelly had last phoned her, so what was she after now?

'Yes, it's me, Kelly,' she verified, trying to inject some enthusiasm into her voice. 'Did you want something?'

'I just thought I'd ring to see how you are,' Kelly cooed.

'Well, that's a first!' Amanda couldn't help commenting.

'There's no need to use that tone, Amanda!' Kelly snapped — but, after a sharp intake of breath, she continued more sweetly, 'It's ages since we saw you, Amanda. I . . . er . . . wondered if you were thinking of coming to see us soon?'

Amanda's eyebrows rose as far as the cucumber gel would allow them. Was she hearing this right?

'We're a bit busy in the hotel at the moment,' she excused herself, while her brain searched for possible reasons for Kelly's unaccustomed geniality. 'Holiday season and all that! Er, is Dad there? Is he keeping well?'

'He's well — but he's in the study with his accountant. I can't disturb him.'

Amanda sighed. She hadn't spoken to her dad in ages. He was always far too busy to come to the phone, Kelly generally excused him when Amanda phoned to maintain contact.

'And the children?' Amanda now asked of her two half-brothers and half-sister — Jack, Rebecca and Thomas.

'They're fine . . . and so am I, since you haven't bothered to ask!' Kelly's voice was sharp again. 'Just as selfish as usual, I note!'

'As you say, Kelly,' Amanda said wearily. 'Is there a purpose to this call? Or did you ring up just to annoy me?'

There was a pause . . . and when

Kelly spoke again, there was a conciliatory note in her voice. 'Now don't let's quarrel, Amanda. Doug has insisted I ring to ask you to come to visit us next week. You can come for three weeks. You did say you haven't booked your holidays yet, didn't you?'

Amanda laughed. 'Are you serious, Kelly? We haven't spent more than one night under the same roof since I left home five years ago! I can't imagine either of us taking any pleasure in each other's company for one day, let alone three weeks!'

'We don't need to! Doug and I won't be here! We're going to America for three weeks.' At Amanda's gasp of incredulity, Kelly hurried on, 'Everything is arranged. We've got our tickets and everything . . . only Charlene has let us down badly and it's too late to make other arrangements. So, we thought of you. I mean, it's not as though you're indispensable at the hotel, are you?'

Amanda could hardly believe her

ears. 'Well, you can think again, Kelly! I might not be indispensable, but I can't take my holiday just like that. Our rosters are arranged a month in advance. You'll have to find someone else to step in for you!'

'Like I said, you're selfish, Amanda! I told Doug you'd never do it! 'Course, he defended you to the hilt! Huh! Just wait 'till I tell him! You have no consideration for others! Don't you care that our holiday will be ruined? And the children! You're always saying you don't see enough of them! And whose fault is that? And, now, here you are, turning down our invitation!'

Amanda closed her eyes, waiting for a lull in the tirade. 'I would like to see the children, Kelly . . . but I can't at such short notice! It just wouldn't be fair to my colleagues! I said I'd take my holiday later so that those with children could have the school holidays.'

There was a short silence and, when Kelly spoke again, it was in an appeasing tone. 'Look, Amanda. It won't be that difficult. Jack is at school and Rebecca goes to nursery every afternoon. There'll only be Thomas to look after all day and you know he's no trouble.'

Amanda sighed heavily, Kelly was missing the point. It just couldn't be done at such short notice!

'Why isn't Charlene willing to do it? I thought she was settling in nicely,' she queried of the latest in a string of nannies. 'I could possibly help her out by giving her a couple of days off each week,' saying 'goodbye' to her days off. Still, it would be nice to see the children again. 'If you pay her a bit extra, I'm sure she'll agree.'

'Charlene has walked out on us, the ungrateful girl. She gave no notice and if she thinks she'll get a reference off me she can think again!'

'Oh.' So, why was that no surprise! 'Well, why don't you try to change your arrangements to the end of September, Kelly? My leave is due then,' Amanda offered, mentally kicking herself for being willing to make the offer. It would make a precedent and Kelly would take more advantage.

'But I don't want to change our holiday! My agent has fixed up some photo shoots. It's all arranged! We're going on Friday,' Kelly snapped. 'Just tell them some urgent family business has cropped up! Anything! What does it matter?'

'It matters to me, Kelly,' Amanda said coldly, totally unmoved by Kelly's pleas.

'Well, don't think this is the last you'll hear of it, Amanda. You'll have your father to deal with, young madam! He'll make you see sense!'

The phone was slammed down.

It was ten minutes later when her father called her number. His voice sounded weary. No doubt he had had ten minutes of Kelly's non-stop complaints about his inconsiderate daughter drumming against his eardrums!

'Can't you do it, Amanda? To please me?'

Amanda hated it when he pleaded like that! Why didn't he stand up to Kelly? Didn't he realise what a fool she made of him?

'She's been looking forward to this trip,' Doug continued. 'We've planned to go to New York, Manhattan and then over to California. Kelly's agent has promised to set up some photo shoots for her. It could be her big lucky break, honey. You know what that means to her!'

Amanda pulled a face and sighed in resignation. She'd known it would happen like this. 'OK, Dad. No promises . . . but I'll see what I can do.'

They chatted for a few more minutes and then said goodbye, leaving Amanda truly deflated. Her night-in was ruined . . . and probably the 'love of her life' ruined, too! Adam, the pastry chef, wouldn't need to look far for someone to step into her shoes! To say nothing of her job! Miss Cartwright would not be pleased.

Miss Cartwight wasn't pleased and

Adam wasn't exactly overjoyed either. 'See you, baby!' had been his parting words. No promise to phone her or visit on his day off.

Amanda travelled by train from Harrogate to St Helens, where her dad met her, looking older than his forty-three years. Amanda held up her face for a kiss and was glad to see some of the lines in his face disappear as he smiled his welcome.

He gave her a swift hug. 'Thanks, Amanda. You're a life-saver! I don't know what I'd have done without you!'

'Do you never think of saying 'No' to Kelly?' she couldn't help asking — then wished she hadn't when she saw the shadow cloud his face.

'I suppose I'm grateful she married an old codger like me. I'm scared of losing her, Amanda. I don't know what I'd do!'

'No-one would ever call you an old codger!' Amanda passionately declared, as she settled herself in the passenger seat, wondering if Kelly had taunted him with the words. She wouldn't put it past her!

She leaned over and squeezed his arm. 'I'm looking forward to seeing the children. Don't you miss them when you go away without them? We had such lovely holidays when Mum was still with us.' Her eyes took on a wistful air as she remembered the happy days spent at the seaside in their holiday cottage in Cornwall. 'It's a pity it's not the school holidays. I could have taken them down there while you're away. They'd have loved it, I'm sure.'

Doug kept his eyes in front as he manoeuvred his way out of the car park. 'I've let it for the season, so it wouldn't have been possible anyway.'

Amanda was surprised. 'Have you? I didn't think you ever let it . . . except to friends for the odd week. You used to say it was your escape-haven! A place to flee to when things got too much.'

'We have the apartment in Spain, now. Didn't I tell you? We share the cost of the household staff with another couple. As you know, Kelly doesn't like self-catering holidays,' he added unnecessarily.

'Gosh, you are living it up, Dad! Your business must be doing well!'

'So-so,' Doug murmured, concentrating on the traffic. 'There's a bit of a recession on at the moment but I'm sure it'll pass.'

Amanda frowned, wondering if she were reading too much into the flicker of anxiety in his voice. He had always had a good business-head on his shoulders.

Fifteen minutes later they were pulling into the sweeping drive of their family home on Higher Lane in Rainford. The houses along this road were all individually built, set well back from the road, with landscaped gardens flourishing to the front and rear of most of the houses — as theirs now did . . . a recent change since Amanda had left home.

Other changes had occurred, too. Gone were all the warm colours her mother had favoured and the stylish wooden furniture. In their place were stark white-painted walls, cream-coloured carpets and chrome-framed furniture with pale cream leather upholstery.

'Cooee!' a voice called over the curving banister rail. 'Is that you, darling?'

Amanda glanced upwards. Kelly, dressed in tight gold lamé pants and the tiniest bikini top, was at the top of the stairs. Her white blonde hair was styled to perfection in a cloud of loose curls about her carefully made-up face. She glided down the stairs into Doug's arms.

'How's my little pussikins?' he greeted her, swinging her off her high-heeled feet and twirling her round.

When her toes were back on the ground, Kelly touched both of Doug's cheeks in turn with hers. 'Mwa! Mwa! Such a horrendous day, darling! I haven't had a minute!' She disentangled herself from one of Doug's arms and turned to Amanda.

'There you are, dear! So lovely to see

you again! You really should come more often, shouldn't she, darling?' turning to smile up at Doug. 'Now, I know Amanda will want time with the children, so I've booked the two of us in for dinner at Chino's. That will give you a clear run of the house, Amanda. I've made a list of their routines for you and you'll find plenty in the fridge for your tea. Now, I simply must get myself ready!' She gave an affected laugh. 'I can't let 'Joe Public' see me at anything other than my best, can I?'

By the time the children were tucked up in bed, Amanda was exhausted! At the risk of making the lounge untidy, she flopped on to the cream leather sofa and breathed out a long sigh. Kids! Who'd have them? She must have aged visibly in the past few hours!

It had begun the minute four-year-old Rebecca realised that both her parents were going out. She had thrown herself on to the floor and kicked and screamed until she was hoarse. Kelly sent her to her room, where she sat stony-faced on the edge of her bed, her arms folded belligerently. She refused to kiss either Doug or Kelly goodbye and, when left alone, scattered the contents of her toy-box about her bedroom floor.

'It was Thomas,' she muttered when Amanda challenged her.

'Hmm, he's a clever baby, then!' Amanda praised.

'No, he's not! He's stupid!'

'Anyway, it wasn't Thomas,' six-year-old Jack announced. 'It was you, Rebecca! It's always you!'

'No, it isn't! You're mean! I hate you!' Rebecca shouted.

'No, you don't,' Amanda pacified her. 'Now, Jack, you go and make sure your room is tidy and Thomas and I will race to see if we can pick up more toys than Rebecca!'

Amanda ignored her. One-year-old Thomas was balanced on her hip, sucking his thumb, oblivious to the tension.

'Come on, Thomas! Ready, steady, go!'

A similar strategy got them through teatime and bath time and by the time Amanda had put Thomas in his cot, read Rebecca's bedtime story, followed by another one for Jack, she felt she had used up her full repertoire of talents and tactics. And if Kelly complained about anything, tough luck!

Amanda's peace was shattered by a tiny hiccup from the doorway. When she twisted round to see who it was, Rebecca's small figure was standing forlornly by the open door.

'I want Mummy to kiss me good-night!' Rebecca whispered. 'She went without kissing me!'

Amanda looked at her in exasperation. 'It was you who wouldn't kiss her!' she pointed out reasonably, as she got to her feet. Seeing Rebecca's unhappy face, she relented. 'Come here for a cuddle before I take you back to bed.'

She drew the little girl on to her lap and stroked back her hair. 'Your mummy will tip-toe in when they get back and she'll kiss you then.'

‘Even if I’m asleep?’

‘Especially if you’re asleep!’ Amanda smiled.

‘And Daddy?’

‘Yes, Daddy, too.’

No sooner was Amanda back downstairs again than the peace of the sitting-room was shattered by the shrill of the telephone. Amanda hurried to pick it up before the sound disturbed the children.

‘Hello?’

‘Hi, Amanda! It’s your dad here. Have the children settled down?’

‘They’re fine, Dad. You’ve no need to worry. You enjoy yourself! Tell Kelly not to forget to kiss Rebecca when you come home. She’s counting on it!’

Amanda was aware of a hesitation in her father’s voice when he spoke.

‘Er . . . it won’t be possible. Kelly thought it best if we leave straight for the airport from here.’

2

'Dad! That's not fair! Rebecca's going to be devastated! She's desperate for a kiss from you both!'

'I know . . . but she does make rather a fuss and Kelly thought . . . that is, we thought . . . it would be best . . . '

'It won't be best, Dad! You just get back here! Where are you?'

'We're on our way to the airport. Our flight goes in just over three hours!'

'What about your luggage?'

'Kelly had it sent ahead this afternoon. I'm sorry, Amanda. I didn't know. Kelly really does think it will be for the best! I'll make it up to them, I promise! I'll buy them all a lovely present . . . and you, too!'

Amanda stood with the phone in her hand long after her father had switched off his mobile. It was a sound from the top of the stairs that finally moved her.

She glanced upwards and could see Rebecca's small figure crouched on the landing. Her thumb was in her mouth and her eyes wide with understanding.

'Was that Daddy?' Rebecca asked.

Amanda paused. What could she say? There was little use lying. 'Yes, darling.'

'Aren't they coming home?'

'Not right now.' She forced some brightness into her voice. 'The time will fly past, Rebecca! They'll be home before you know it!'

'They didn't kiss me! They'll never come back! I know it! And I don't care!'

With a deep sob, Rebecca turned and fled back to her room.

Rebecca woke three times during the night. Each time she sobbed inconsolably until sleep overcame her. After the second time, Amanda decided it would be best if she lay alongside her, which is what she did.

Her broken sleep didn't refresh her and she was awakened by Thomas shouting, 'Mummy!' As soon as her eyes opened, she knew she had overslept.

A glance at the clock confirmed it. It was past eight o'clock. She'd never get Jack to school on time! She carefully slipped out of bed and padded into the nursery, where Thomas was bouncing in his cot, beaming at her. Amanda lifted him out and kissed him.

Jack was still fast asleep. Amanda hurriedly woke him up and told him to get himself washed and dressed whilst she saw to Thomas. She'd leave Rebecca as long as she could.

She changed Thomas's nappy and hurried downstairs with him and sat him in his high chair. A glance in the fridge showed that there was one bottle of milk prepared for him. She popped it in the bottle warmer and started looking for the cereal packets. All the cupboards looked the same. Where was everything?

Thankfully Jack appeared downstairs. With his help, she managed to get breakfast under way. Once she had fed Thomas and hastily buttered a piece of toast for herself, she ran upstairs to waken Rebecca.

'I'm tired! I want my mummy!' Rebecca wailed.

'I know, love, but she's not here. You know she'd gone on holiday with Daddy.'

'I wanted to go, too! Why couldn't we all go? It's not fair!'

'Maybe it's not. Now come to the bathroom so I can wash your face and get you dressed. We're running late this morning. I've put out some clothes on the end of your bed for you to put on.'

Having successfully delivered Jack to school, Amanda returned home to sort out the remnants of breakfast and try to get organised. Rebecca wanted to do some colouring and Thomas was soon ready for his morning nap. The sound of a key in the lock heralded the entrance of a pleasant-looking lady of middle years.

'Marlene Murphy, dear. I come every day but Sunday,' she told Amanda. 'Didn't Mrs Purvey tell you? I do general housework and make the evening meal.'

Had Kelly told her? Amanda couldn't honestly remember. She didn't think so. At least she wasn't expected to run the whole household, then! Partway through the morning, Mrs Murphy noticed Jack's lunch box in a cupboard and Amanda realised she hadn't made up a packed lunch for him. Whilst Mrs Murphy made some sandwiches and put them in the box with a pear and a pot of yoghurt, Amanda woke Thomas and got him ready to go out again.

'We'll go to the playpark after,' she promised Rebecca, forestalling a rebellious refusal.

Thankfully, Rebecca agreed and willingly changed out of her ballet dress and they hurried off to deliver the lunchbox to Jack before he missed it. The promised visit to the park went well and Amanda began to hope that Rebecca had accepted her mother's absence. They hadn't been back in the house long when the phone rang. Amanda crossed the room to pick it up. It was Kelly.

'Hello, Amanda. Is Rebecca there?'

'Yes. Just a minute.' She held the phone towards Rebecca. 'It's Mummy, Rebecca. Come and say hello.'

Rebecca scowled and folded her arms, sitting down on the floor with a thump. She jerked her folded arms on to her crossed legs and jutted out her lower lip.

Rebecca refused to move. When Amanda carried the phone across to her, Rebecca leaped to her feet and ran from the room.

'I won't! I won't! I won't!'

Amanda spoke into the phone. 'I'm sorry, Kelly. She's run upstairs.'

'Then go after her and make her speak to me!'

Amanda took the phone upstairs but Rebecca had slammed shut her door and was kicking it from the other side, screaming, 'No! No! No!'

'I'm sorry, Kelly. You can hear the noise. I'll put Thomas on. It's Mummy, Thomas! Say Mamma!'

'Mamm . . . mam . . . mamm!'

Amanda spoke into the phone. 'I'll ring you back, Kelly, when Rebecca comes down. Your number's programmed in, I suppose?'

'That's no use!' Kelly snapped. 'I'm at a fashion show and it's about to begin. We've been told to switch our cell phones off.'

And the phone went dead.

Two minutes after Amanda put the phone down, Rebecca crept back into the living room. 'I'll speak to Mummy now,' she said quietly.

'Oh, Rebecca! She's gone!'

Over lunch, Rebecca sulked defiantly and Amanda marvelled that she managed to get her to her nursery at Crank Village without having to resort to bribery. After school, the mother of a little girl called Lucy asked if Rebecca could have tea at her house and, discovering that this was an established custom for Friday evening, Amanda agreed.

She tried to ring Kelly so that Jack could speak to her, but her phone was still switched off. She tried her father's phone, but the same there. She couldn't imagine her father enjoying a fashion show, but her dad seemed to go along with whatever Kelly told him these days.

Teatime with Jack and Thomas passed pleasantly and Amanda managed to contact Kelly to allow Jack to speak to his parents.

'But I insist on speaking to Rebecca when she comes home, Amanda,' Kelly said sharply. 'I need to know my little girl still loves me!'

Amanda agreed but she had bathed Thomas and put him to bed before Rebecca arrived home. The little girl was worn out and had fallen asleep in the car during the short journey home. Not wanting a repeat of previous confrontations, Amanda decided against waking her to try to persuade her to speak to her mother and managed to undress her and get her into her pyjamas and into bed without really waking her. She read Jack a bedtime story and settled him down to sleep.

'Dad said I'm the man of the house while he's away,' he told Amanda as she leaned over to kiss him goodnight. 'But he said you'd help me. You will, won't you?'

'Of course I will. That's why I'm here!'

It was half-past-ten when Kelly telephoned. In spite of Kelly's insistence that she waken her daughter and make her talk to her on the phone, she refused to do so.

'She's been upset and didn't sleep much last night, Kelly. She needs to catch up on her sleep. I'll get her to ring you tomorrow about lunchtime. That should allow for the time difference,' Amanda promised.

'Don't be ridiculous, Amanda! I'll probably still be in bed! My work keeps me up late, you know! It's not just a holiday! You really ought to be more considerate!'

And with that, Kelly slammed down the phone.

Saturday morning, breakfast was a more leisurely affair and both Jack and Rebecca played in the playroom because it was drizzling. Jack was building a complex Lego construction and Rebecca played at tea-parties with her dolls.

The sky brightened after lunch, and Amanda took the children to the play area for an hour or so and then let Jack and Rebecca choose a treat from the newsagents on Church Road to eat on their way home. Thomas had enjoyed the swing and was now getting fractious, so Amanda sat on the floor to play with him. Seeing that Thomas was getting all the attention, Rebecca began to skip around the room, knocking over Jack's Lego.

'Aw, Rebecca! You've ruined it!' Jack shouted. 'Amanda, tell her to stop! Give that back to me! I need that piece!'

In exasperation, Amanda put Thomas on to his play mat, gave him a toy to hold and then tried to stop Rebecca from scattering yet more Lego all over the floor.

'This is very naughty of you, Rebecca!' she said sharply. 'Just give that piece back to Jack! And then you can pick all the rest up!'

'Shan't! Shan't! It's a silly boy's game!'

'Yes, you will!'

Amanda grabbed at the piece Rebecca was holding high in her hand but missed as Rebecca whirled away, jumping up and down on the Lego, laughing excitedly. Amanda grabbed hold of her arm, pulling her away but Rebecca wasn't finished yet. She began to flail her arms wildly.

Trying to restrain the now-hysterical child, Amanda swept her up into her arms. Thomas began to cry and Amanda felt herself to be on the point of cracking up. Two nights of broken sleep didn't help and she now felt at the end of her tether.

'Rebecca! Stop this at once!' She knew her voice was rising higher than usual but she really couldn't help it. 'Do you hear me? Stop it before I . . . '

'Before you what?' a male voice asked

from behind her.

Amanda whirled round. A tall, athletic looking man in the doorway. He was smartly dressed in a pale grey lightweight summer suit. His hair was dark brown and his eyes the colour of chocolate. If the eyes had been smiling, Amanda knew she would have melted into them . . . but they weren't smiling. The look behind them was as cold as steel.

Rebecca slipped out of Amanda's slackened grasp. 'Uncle Simon!' she called, running headlong into him. 'Amanda's being nasty to me . . . and I hate her!'

Amanda wished the ground would open up and swallow her whole. She hadn't seen Simon since her father's wedding, seven years ago . . . but he had the same effect on her now as he had then! She narrowed her eyes to strip seven years from his suave business-man's veneer. He'd been eighteen, while she was a gawky thirteen-year-old who had admired his good looks from afar.

He hadn't paid any attention to her and probably had no idea who she was.

She felt hot and flustered after trying to control Rebecca's behaviour and ran her hand through her hair. What a time for him to come! Why couldn't he have come at a time when she had everything under control? Rebecca's words hadn't been lost to her either . . . though if Simon knew his niece well, he wouldn't take her all that seriously! And why was he here anyway? Didn't he know that Kelly and her father had gone to America?

She decided that the best approach would be to greet him warmly and ask questions afterwards, so she thrust out her hand.

'Hi, Simon! I don't know if you remember me. I'm Amanda, Doug's eldest daughter. We've not met since their wedding, have we?'

Simon didn't take hold of her hand. He ignored it and swooped his niece into his arms as if she were as light as thistledown.

‘I know who you are!’ he said coldly, his voice speaking more huskily than she remembered. ‘I’m not surprised that Kelly is out of her mind with worry, if that charming little scene I interrupted is anything to go by! You’re obviously unfit to be left in control of young children!’

Amanda felt her cheeks flushing even darker than before. She knew she had been on the verge of thoroughly losing her temper with Rebecca but she had remained in control of it, in spite of the aggravation. She felt annoyed at his all-too-ready assumption that she was at fault.

Jack scrambled to his feet. ‘Hi, Uncle Simon. Will you help me rebuild my air base?’

‘Hi, Jack! Give me five!’ The two of them slapped palms and Simon added, ‘Yes, just give me a minute to sort this out first.’

Rebecca nestled her head into Simon’s shoulder and was peeping under her lashes at Amanda’s discomfort. Amanda shot her a look of exasperation.

'I know I sounded cross at her — but look at the mess she's made of Jack's Lego! And it all needs tidying up! So, you can stop all this play-acting, Rebecca and come and help to do it.'

Amanda made a move towards Rebecca, who immediately scrabbled further up Simon's body.

'Don't you dare lay a finger on my niece!' Simon warned hoarsely. 'She is obviously scared stiff of you!'

'Your niece is my sister!' Amanda retorted. 'And she's not scared of me! She's done nothing but play-up ever since Dad and Kelly left so abruptly without even saying goodbye!'

'A fact you have played upon by refusing to let her speak to her mother!'

Amanda's mouth opened and closed with no sound coming out, the absurdity of the statement taking her breath away.

'I've done no such thing!' she eventually got out. She remembered Kelly's call the previous evening when

Rebecca was in bed. 'Well, only in as far as . . . '

'Did you or did you not refuse to bring Rebecca to the phone last night?'

'Yes . . . but only because it was so late and she was fast asleep.'

'You had no right to prevent her talking to her mother! She's only four and is missing her parents.'

'I know perfectly well how old she is!'

'You obviously don't know how to handle her!'

As Amanda glared at Simon, Thomas started to cry. 'Fine!' she said tightly, bending down to pick up the baby. 'You 'handle' Rebecca . . . and get her to help sort all this out! I'll see to Thomas.' And, with her head held high and her back rigid with as much dignity as she could muster, she stalked out of the room and into the kitchen.

3

She hadn't been going to give Thomas his bottle quite so soon but it seemed the best way to calm him down, upset as he was with all the shouting. When he'd taken all the milk he was going to, she sat him in his high chair, gave him a rusk to chew on and went back to the playroom. Simon was straightening up from his position on the floor. Amanda looked pointedly at the box of Lego in his hand.

'I see how persuasive you are!' she said, hating herself for resorting to sarcasm but couldn't think of any other way to express herself. With immediate contrition, she held out her hand for the box. 'I'll see to the rest. Come on, Rebecca. Tell Jack you're sorry.'

Rebecca pouted at that but, after looking at Amanda's determined expression, she did as she was bidden.

Her tantrum forgotten, Rebecca skipped upstairs and Amanda returned to the kitchen, followed by Simon. He sank on to one of the stools by the breakfast bar and seemed more like the eighteen-year-old she had remembered for so long. Amanda noticed for the first time how tired he looked.

'Have you travelled far today?' she asked, hoping he would respond to her conciliatory tone.

'I've just flown in from America.'

His voice was no more than a croak and he passed the back of his hand wearily across his forehead. 'I'm fair whacked. It's been a busy week . . . and I think I've picked up some bug or other.'

He looked so woebegone that Amanda felt her annoyance at him slipping away.

'You could do with drinking a hot lemon powder . . . and then having a good sleep from the look of you. Where are you staying?'

Simon managed a wry grin. 'Here?'

'Oh!'

Well, it was only to be expected. He had probably stayed here more than she had in recent years, if Rebecca's reaction was anything to go by.

'Is that a problem?' Simon croaked.

'N . . . no, of course not!'

She wasn't a hundred per cent sure that that statement was true. She could envisage problems all round . . . a clash of personalities, a clash of interest, a clash of hormones — because, in spite of his unsympathetic attitude displayed so far, she couldn't rid herself of the romantic fantasies she had woven around Simon in her teenage years from that one week leading up to the wedding. She had better get a firm grip on herself and keep her fantasies where they belonged . . . in the past!

Simon was visibly wilting in front of her and she felt a surge of alarm. 'Look, I'll put the kettle on and go and get your bags out of the car. You did drive here, did you? Or did you come by taxi?' she added as she plugged in the kettle.

'Car.'

He stood up and fumbled in his pocket for his keys . . . and dropped them on to the floor. Amanda bent down to pick them up and encountered Simon's fingers as he groped on the floor. The touch of his fingers seemed to burn her and she snatched her hand away . . . but Simon didn't appear to notice.

'Can you get upstairs by yourself?' she asked quickly, to cover her confusion. 'Where do you normally sleep?'

'In my bedroom.'

Was he being funny? A look at his face convinced her otherwise.

'OK. Well, you get up there and I'll be with you as soon as I can.'

She got Simon's flight bag from his car and returned indoors. The kettle had boiled and she quickly made a hot lemon drink. She slung the flight bag over her shoulder and picked up the mug. Rebecca was clattering down the stairs with an armful of dolls.

'Be careful,' Amanda warned automatically. She waited until Rebecca had reached the hall before going up.

'Uncle Simon's in your bed,' Rebecca told her.

'Oh!'

Still, it was probably the one he normally used and likely the only one made up . . . and in Simon's current state he needed to be somewhere familiar for bathroom purposes.

She paused in the doorway. Simon lay flat on his back under the light-weight duvet. His suit was draped over a chair, his socks and shoes underneath it and his shirt was on the end of the bed. Was he asleep already?

She let the flight bag slip off her shoulder and lowered it to the floor before tiptoeing over to peer at his face. Apart from being flushed, he was sleeping peacefully. A curl of his hair lay plastered to his forehead and, without thinking, she reached out and smoothed it to one side. His eyes shot open, catching her by surprise.

She needn't have worried. He simply stared uncomprehendingly at her. His face creased into perplexion but he didn't move.

'You're very hot,' Amanda commented, as if to excuse her touching him. 'You need to drink this.'

She put the mug of hot lemon on the bedside table and slid her arm around his back. Sensing what was required of him, Simon struggled to raise himself and Amanda held the mug to his lips. His well-muscled chest glistened with sweat and his tan showed that he had holidayed abroad. When the mug was empty, she lowered his head and shoulders back to the bed and covered him with the duvet again. Deciding to telephone the doctor's surgery for advice, she ran downstairs and made the call.

The receptionist reassured her that she was doing all she could for the time being and promised that the doctor would call later.

The doctor came just before the children's bath time and confirmed that Simon was suffering from a viral infection.

'If he gets any worse, don't hesitate to call me out,' she told Amanda. 'Apart from that, give him plenty of fluids and here's a prescription for pain killers.' She looked at the three children. 'Since you've got your hands full, I'll pop it into the pharmacy on my way back to the medical centre and one of them will bring it out for you. Bye for now!'

Amanda was greatly reassured by the doctor's visit and now felt that she could cope with the added responsibility of a bed-confined patient. She went to the bathroom and ran the water for the children's bath. Thomas was bathed and was playing happily on the bathroom floor whilst Rebecca took her turn in the water. She was still in the bath when the phone rang. Hoping it was her dad or Kelly, Amanda hastily scooped Rebecca out of the bath and pulled up the plug.

'Quick! Wrap the towel around you, Rebecca! We'll take it in Mummy and Daddy's bedroom.'

'Is it Mummy or Daddy?'

'I expect so. Come on.'

Amanda fervently hoped she were right. She wasn't sure how Rebecca would react if she weren't! To her relief, she was!

'Hi, Amanda!' her dad's voice came clearly down the line. 'Everything going OK?'

'Yes, fine, Dad. How are you?'

'Just fine! We have a hectic schedule but Kelly's on top of the world! She's hoping some sort of contract will come from it all. What's that?' The line went quiet for a moment whilst Doug responded to whatever Kelly had said to him. 'I'll put Kelly on now,' he came back with. 'Are the children all right?'

'They're fine, Dad. They were just having their bath. Here's Rebecca.'

She gave the receiver to Rebecca, who listened intently but didn't say any words. Kelly was obviously asking questions because Rebecca was nodding her head.

'Speak to your mummy, Rebecca,' Amanda encouraged her. 'She wants to hear your voice.' She moved her face nearer to the phone. 'She's nodding and smiling, Kelly,' she spoke into the receiver. 'Pardon . . . ? No, of course I'm not!'

Her face whitened. Why did Kelly always think the worst of her? Just as if she would prevent Rebecca from speaking! She put the receiver back against Rebecca's ear and smiled encouragingly, laying aside her annoyance with Kelly.

'Tell Mummy about the tea party, Rebecca.'

After a slight hesitation, Rebecca whispered, 'We had a tea party, Mummy . . . but we didn't make a mess, did we, Amanda?'

'No. You were fine! Tell Mummy Jack and Thomas enjoyed it, too.'

Rebecca repeated the words and then listened again, shaking her head. 'No, it was on the floor . . . but we tidied everything up.'

After a few moments, Rebecca held out the phone to Amanda. 'Mummy wants to speak to Jack now.'

Jack chatted for a few minutes, telling her that Uncle Simon was here now. After a pause he added. 'I can't. He's in bed.' He listened again and then looked at Amanda. 'Can I go and waken him?'

Amanda shook her head. 'No. Best not. Here, give me the phone. Hi, Kelly! . . . What? Don't be ridiculous! . . . Of course I'm not! Kelly, stop saying such nonsense and listen, will you? Simon's not well. He's got some sort of viral infection . . . Yes, the doctor's been and he's to stay in bed . . . Right.'

She put the receiver to Thomas's ear and watched the baby's face as he recognised his mother's voice.

'Mammamam!' Thomas babbled, bouncing up and down in Amanda's arms.

Eventually, Amanda heard her father's voice speaking and bent her head to listen. He was speaking to Thomas and then said, 'Amanda?'

'Yes, I'm here!'

'Kelly's got a busy schedule but I'll

make sure we phone again sometime tomorrow. Thanks for all you're doing, love! Take care. Kiss my babies for me!'

Rebecca looked a bit downcast when the phone was put down again. 'Well, that was nice, wasn't it?' Amanda said cheerfully. 'Mummy and Daddy are enjoying their holiday and are missing you very much. And they send you a big kiss. Here it is!'

'Why couldn't we go?' Rebecca wanted to know after Amanda had kissed her.

'It's a very busy holiday. Not the sort where you would have time to play. Mummy hopes to get some modelling work from it. You know, like the ladies in Mummy's fashion magazines. You'd like to see Mummy in a magazine, wouldn't you?'

'Mmm, I s'pose.'

'I tell you what,' Amanda said, seizing upon an inspiration. 'Tomorrow, we'll cut some pictures out of some magazines and make up some pages of what we'd like Mummy to do. And, we could scan some photos of her into the computer and make the pictures actually look like Mummy!'

The children settled down easily after a bedtime story and Amanda searched for photographs of Kelly to scan into the computer, getting a few likely images ready for the following day.

About an hour later, the phone went again. Amanda sighed in exasperation. What now? However, although it was a female voice, it wasn't Kelly.

'Hello. It's Nicola Weston here,' the voice said. 'May I speak to Simon, please? He is there, isn't he? Only he said he would call me and he hasn't.'

'Yes, he's here, Nicola but he's in bed . . . asleep.'

'Can't you waken him?'

'I'd rather not. Can I take a message to give him when he wakes up?'

'I suppose so . . . but I'd rather speak to him myself. I'm his partner and I want to know when I'll be seeing him.'

'Oh!'

Amanda hoped her disappointment

wasn't evident in her voice, though she shouldn't have been surprised to learn he had a partner, she reasoned. After all, he had all the desirable traits a man should have. Lucky Nicola!

'I'm afraid he's got some kind of viral infection,' Amanda explained, trying to suppress her jealous thoughts, thankful that she had learned of Simon's relationship with Nicola before he had had time to suspect her own resurging feelings for him. 'He's running a high temperature and the doctor recommends bed rest for a few days.'

'Oh! I'm not sure I should come and see him,' Nicola said hesitantly. 'Is he infectious? I mean, it's a bit risky, isn't it? Viruses can be quite awful.'

'I suppose the risk depends on how badly you want to see him.'

'Hmm. Maybe I'd better leave it a day or two. Tell him I called, won't you?'

Amanda pursed her lips as she replaced the phone. She might have known Simon would have someone!

She went upstairs and looked in on Simon. His breathing was a bit ragged but the doctor had assured her that it would be a sign that he was fighting the infection, so she wasn't alarmed by it. She made him another drink and helped him to drink it.

'My head hurts!' he croaked hoarsely.

Amanda had popped two painkillers into the mug of warm water.

'Drink this!' she commanded, holding it to his lips as he gulped it down. She wiped his lips and chin with a tissue, relieved when he sank back on the pillows.

'By the way, Nicola phoned,' she told him.

'Uh? Oh . . . great.' And he went straight back to sleep.

4

Amanda awoke the next day feeling full of energy. It was Sunday. No Mrs Murphy today. She'd have to do everything herself.

Her first priority was to look in on Simon. He seemed as though he had had a restless night but was softly snoring when she looked into his room.

She showered and dressed and saw to the children's breakfasts before returning to rouse him. His chin was covered in dark stubble and dark rings were under his eyes. He was still in no condition to sit up and eat anything so she spent the day alternately playing with the children and popping upstairs to keep him supplied with drinks and sponging his upper body. On one occasion, she encountered him staggering along to the bathroom but she wasn't sure he even noticed her presence.

In spite of having an extra guest to take care of, Sunday passed pleasantly. In the evening, remembering the fiasco of Friday morning's school run, Amanda got everything prepared for Monday morning before she went to bed.

After she returned from taking Jack to school, she took a bowl of warm water into Simon's room to wipe his face. At the touch of the cloth, he opened his eyes and glared at her.

'What do you think you're doing?' he asked sharply.

Amanda flinched at his sharp tone. 'You've been quite unwell, I'm cooling you down.'

He pushed her hand away. 'I'm perfectly well, thank you. If you don't mind, I'm getting up!'

She stepped back and watched him with folded arms as he sat up and tried to swing his legs over the side of the bed. He swayed and looked visibly queasy.

He groaned. 'I feel awful! What's the matter with me?'

'The doctor said it was a viral infection. You've had a fever, a headache and a sore throat.'

'Oh, I suppose I have to thank you for taking care of me?'

Amanda felt a surge of anger at his apparent attitude.

'Oh, and Nicola phoned. She wants to know when you're going home.'

'Home?'

'Wherever it is you and Nicola live, I suppose!'

He looked at her with narrowed eyes. 'Er, what exactly did Nicola say?'

'Just that she is your 'partner' and, when you're not infectious, she'll gladly accept you back . . . or words to that effect! Not exactly a Florence Nightingale, is she?'

'No, I don't think nursing the sick is among her accomplishments,' he said ruefully. 'Still, you can't have it all, can you?'

Simon lay back on his pillows and tried to go back to sleep. In spite of his assurances that he felt a lot better, he knew he was nothing like recovered. He needed to get in touch with Nicola . . . but it was too much effort to get out his mobile phone and his brain was incapable of making a fluent sentence.

The house seemed quiet most of the day, though at times he could hear a pleasant voice drifting up from the garden and the humming sound of a vacuum cleaner somewhere in the house. He thought of Amanda, trying to match up her present appearance with the rather coltish thirteen-year-old who had followed him around with adoring eyes when he had spent a week here before Kelly and Doug were married.

Later, Rebecca and Jack drifted in to see him. He wished he felt able to respond to them but had to admit he felt grateful when Amanda shooed them downstairs.

After a light omelette for tea, Simon felt much strengthened. He carefully made his way to the bathroom and enjoyed a warm shower.

As he paused by the top of the stairs,

he could hear Rebecca talking and realised she was speaking on the telephone.

'And Uncle Simon is sleeping in Amanda's bed and . . . '

'Give that phone to me, Rebecca!' he heard Amanda say indignantly. 'Are you still there, Kelly? . . . No, of course not! . . . No, I know she doesn't tell lies. No oftener than any other child, anyway. Simon just happens to have . . . Oh, for goodness sake, Kelly! . . . No, I won't go and get him! He's fast asleep and you'll just have to take my word for it! . . . No, you probably don't but it's all you're going to get for the time being! Is my father there? . . . Well, I'd like to speak to him, if you don't mind.'

Simon heard Amanda's voice quieten down and he grinned to himself as he made his way back to his bedroom . . . Amanda's bedroom, he corrected himself. Kelly seemed to have met her match in her stepdaughter. Was that why the fur always flew when they met together? Were they too similar in character? He grimaced, knowing his sister could be a bit of a shrew at times. Was Amanda the same?

The following morning, he awoke feeling almost as bright as a summer's day. He got out of bed and pulled the curtains wide apart, taking a deep breath of fresh air as his outstretched arms opened up his chest. After wanting only to be allowed to curl up and die for a few days, it was suddenly very good to be alive!

The sheer joy of shaving away three days' growth of beard remarkably improved his humour and he was humming a tune by the time he returned to his bedroom. Once dressed, he gathered up his discarded clothes and made his way downstairs.

Amanda was spoon-feeding Thomas with some white gooey stuff, her hand poised as she glared sideways at Rebecca.

'I've told you, I've already put sugar on it! It's dissolved in the milk . . . that's why you can't see it!'

Rebecca peered at her Weetabix.

'No, it's not! There's none there! Anyway, Charlene lets me put on my own sugar!' She pushed her dish away and belligerently folded her arms, a look of defiance on her face.

Amanda spooned some goo into Thomas's mouth. 'And I saw how much you took yesterday!' she retorted, not even looking round. 'Eat it or leave it, Rebecca. You'll get nothing else until it's gone, though!'

Simon felt himself bristling. Did she never let the children make any choices? He thought it time he advertised his presence.

'Good morning, ladies! Lovely day, isn't it?'

Amanda turned round. Her cheeks reddened slightly and she seemed to be taken unawares by his sudden appearance. Nevertheless, she smiled brightly. 'Oh, good morning, Simon! How are you feeling today?'

For a moment, his heart leapt at the warmth in her eyes but he pushed the feeling aside. It wouldn't do to get too friendly. Not until he was clear about how things were between her and the children.

'Much better, thanks. Alive and ravenous!'

'Good! I was going to bring you a breakfast tray.'

Simon followed her glance to where a prepared tray lay on the worktop. 'That's all right, thank you. I'll eat it here. Er, where can I put these for . . . er . . . Mrs . . . ?' Simon glanced apologetically at the pile of clothes in his arms, searching his memory for the name of the domestic help, wishing he didn't still feel thirty degrees below par.

'Mrs Murphy's not in yet. Put them by the door and I'll take them to the laundry room in a minute.'

'It's all right. I'll take them,' he said stiffly, not wanting to be beholden to her.

Amanda shrugged. 'Please yourself. Then come and get on with your breakfast. I've to take Jake to school soon.'

'I want some sugar, Uncle Simon!' Rebecca demanded, as soon as he sat down.

'Do you now? Isn't there a little word needed?'

Rebecca beamed at him. 'Please!'

'That's better!' he praised, pushing the sugar bowl towards her.

'I've already said 'no'!' Amanda objected.

'You're too hard on her! What's a bit of sugar?'

Rebecca grinned triumphantly and dug in her spoon, scooping up a full load, which she immediately deposited on to her Weetabix. She reached forward again, to scoop another spoonful.

'Hey! That's enough!' Simon remonstrated quickly, reaching for the sugar bowl, accidentally knocking the spoon sideways. His arm caught the small milk jug, knocking it over, the milk flowing across the table into the scattered sugar. 'Now, see what you've done!'

'No, I didn't! You knocked me!'

Amanda looked round at the mess and cast her eyes towards the ceiling. Simon felt himself getting defensive but Amanda merely resumed feeding Thomas. 'You'll find a cloth by the sink,' she told him.

Feeling chastened, Simon got the cloth and made an attempt to wipe up the milk and sugar. 'I'm not used to dealing with children,' he excused himself, recognising how feeble he sounded.

'Join the club!' Amanda invited, an eyebrow raised sardonically.

Simon had to admit that she had a point. How old was she? About twenty? Maybe he was being too harsh on her?

The rest of the breakfast time passed amicably enough. The domestic atmosphere was surprisingly pleasant and Simon reflected that normally on his infrequent visit to his sister's home, he and Kelly, and Doug if he were around, breakfasted separately from the children. It was his first experience of 'behind the scenes'. Not the time or place for reading his daily newspaper, he swiftly surmised!

And, once breakfast was over, and Amanda was busily getting the children ready to take Jack to school, the resulting noisy activity made his head buzz.

It was quiet after they had gone. Eventually, Simon went downstairs again, made another mug of coffee and telephoned Nicola, explaining what had happened and telling her he'd be taking the week off work for recuperation. He discussed a few things with her and ended the call, happy to have a few days of unexpected leave.

Mrs Murphy arrived and set herself busy with clearing away the breakfast dishes and Simon settled himself in the spacious sun-lounge that was built on to the back of the house. His sister had done very well for herself, he reflected. Doug obviously loved her and enjoyed spoiling her and although she frequently complained to him about Amanda's insolent attitude towards her, he was beginning to think his sister had judged her harshly.

The telephone rang, disturbing his tranquillity. He had better answer it. It might be Kelly or Doug. He would be able to reassure them that everything was fine and that they had no need to worry.

Light-heartedly, he picked up the receiver. As he listened to the speaker at the other end of the line, his face changed colour and when he had replaced the receiver, he sank on to the settee with his head in his hands.

Simon dreaded Amanda's return home with the children. How would they take it? How could he soften the blow?

The time seemed interminable until he heard the sounds that signalled their return. He pulled himself to his feet and went with a heavy heart towards the kitchen.

'I want baked beans and toast!' Rebecca was saying. 'And Thomas likes baby beans and toast. I'll show you where they are.'

She skipped into the kitchen, leaving the door wide open so that Amanda could lift Thomas out of the pushchair and carry him in. Amanda smiled at him over Rebecca's head.

'Hello. Did you think we'd got lost? It's such a lovely day, I hadn't the heart to bring them back too soon! Have you managed to . . . '

Her voice tailed away as she took in the expression on his face.

'What is it? What's happened?'

Simon stepped forward to take hold of her hands but she back away, her eyes wide with apprehension.

'I'm sorry, Amanda. I need to speak to you on your own?'

'Why? What's happened? Tell me!'

He couldn't! Not with Rebecca listening so attentively. 'Er . . . there's a drink of orange juice on the table in the sun-lounge, Rebecca . . . and some biscuits,' he added as she hesitated to leave them.

Reluctantly, Rebecca trailed sideways

out of the kitchen. Her face showed she knew something had happened to upset him but the lure of orange juice and biscuits over-rode her curiosity.

When she had gone, he knew he had no further excuse for delay. He looked away, through the window into the lovely garden, seeking the right words but failed to find inspiration.

'There's no easy way to say this, Amanda,' he said softly. 'I'm afraid there's been an accident. Kelly and your father . . . they're . . . '

He wished he could say, 'badly injured', but he couldn't.

' . . . They're dead.'

5

Amanda heard the words but couldn't take in the meaning. 'No! No! You've got it wrong! How can they be? We were talking to them only last night.'

She was backing away from Simon. In some foolish way, she felt that if she didn't let him touch her, his words couldn't harm her . . . but they were already searing through her like a hot knife!

'I'm sorry, Amanda. There was a phone call from a man at the British Embassy. He said there'd been a terrible accident. A multiple pile-up on one of the expressways.'

Amanda put her hands to her head. She could feel her blood pounding through her veins and felt that her head would explode with the force of it.

'No. It can't be true. There's been a mistake.'

Rebecca ran back into the kitchen, a

partly-eaten biscuit clutched in her hand.

'What's the matter, Amanda? Why are you crying?'

'I'm not crying,' Amanda denied. But when she put her hand to her cheek, it came away wet with tears. Her facial muscles weren't under her control and she knew her face was distorted by shock and grief. Although she desperately wanted Simon's words to be false, she knew they weren't. But, oh, it was hard to accept!

Rebecca was clutching her legs, crying because she was, but not sure why. Amanda dropped to her knees and hugged her tightly.

'It's all right, Rebecca! It's all right!' Though she knew it wasn't.

Her anguished eyes locked with Simon's. His face looked frozen with shock. What were they to do? How were they to tell Rebecca and Jack that their mummy and daddy wouldn't be coming home?

'One of us has to fly out to America to . . . to identify them.'

Simon's words were quietly spoken

but they seemed to resonate in her head. She looked at him, panic-stricken, still unable to fully take it in.

'What about the children?' she whispered. How could she leave them?

'I'll go to America,' Simon offered at once. There was no way he could put Amanda through that.

Amanda found herself clutching Rebecca, as if the solid feeling of her closeness kept her from collapsing. 'How long is that likely to take?'

Simon shrugged. 'It depends on the findings at the inquest, if there was any negligence or dangerous driving etc. The embassy guy said sometimes it's only a week. Other times it takes much longer. Each state has its own rules and regulations.'

Simon booked his flight over the phone. He would fly out tomorrow evening. He then telephoned the Health Centre to ask for advice about how to break the news to Jack and Rebecca. The receptionist promised to contact a Childcare Therapist who, hopefully, would be able to visit them that evening. He then telephoned *Gornall's* the local funeral director's office in Cross Pit Lane and made an appointment to see them that afternoon.

The day passed in a blur. Somehow, Amanda managed to take Rebecca to her nursery and had a quiet word with the head teacher, explaining what had happened. Mrs Anderson said she would sort out someone to take Rebecca home at the end of the afternoon. When she arrived home, she phoned Jack's school and was grateful when the same suggestion was made. It gave them a few hours' respite and time to compose their thoughts.

The Childcare Counsellor came and suggested ways of breaking the news to Jack and Rebecca, stressing a loving environment and plenty of reassurance.

'It will have to be before their bodies are flown home,' she advised. 'They will need to grieve with you. It will be part of their healing. Don't deny them it. Wrap yourselves around them and be their family. Children are very resilient, you know.' She looked from one to the other. 'Have you made any long-term plans for their future, yet?'

'I'll look after them, of course!' they both replied together.

'They're my nephews and niece!' Simon added.

'They're my brothers and sister!' Amanda protested.

'Half-brothers and sister!' Simon corrected.

Amanda glared at him. 'This is my childhood home. Are you going to throw me out of it?'

'Don't fight over it,' the counsellor said softly. 'Your nerves are particularly raw at present. Give each other space.'

They agreed to keep them both off school the following day and ask Mrs Murphy to take Thomas to the park, so that they could give all their attention to Jack and Rebecca.

They listened; they cried, they clung to Amanda.

'I didn't kiss them goodbye!' Rebecca remembered with a sob.

'Your mummy and daddy knew you loved them,' Simon said.

'Will we never see them again?' Jack asked quietly, wiping the back of his hand across his eyes.

Amanda shook her head. 'No. I'm sorry. None of us will.'

Amanda hugged them and then held them away from her so that she could see their faces. 'When my nana died, my mummy told me that every time I feel a sunbeam on my face, it's like a kiss from my nanna.'

'It means we'll never forget them, doesn't it?' Jack whispered.

'Yes . . . and you'll be able to tell Thomas about them as he gets older.'

'Yes. Can I go and play now?' Rebecca asked.

'Yes, of course you can.'

Rebecca slipped off Amanda's lap and went upstairs to her room to get her toys out.

'What about you, Jack? What do you want to do?'

'I want to stay here with you and

Uncle Simon. Can I sit on your knee now that Rebecca's gone upstairs?'

'Of course you can. Come on!'

It was a difficult day. One that Amanda hoped never to experience again. The sadness hung in the air and tears were never far from any of them. To Amanda, it seemed as though Simon had the best control but she presumed he was suffering within. The British stiff upper lip, she supposed, thankful that, as a female, she could cry without feeling any shame.

Later, when the children were finally tucked up in bed, Amanda and Simon sat exhausted in the living-room. Amanda wished she were able to take sanctuary in his arms; lay her head on his chest; to feel his arms around her and his hands soothingly stroking her hair. She needed to hear him . . . someone . . . anyone . . . whisper that she had no need to worry, that he would take care of everything, that he would always be there for her . . . words that she had used to console Jack and Rebecca.

Even without knowing her thoughts, Simon looked embarrassed, as if he didn't know what to say or do. He finally reached out and took hold of Amanda's hand and squeezed it reassuringly. Amanda thought he was about to say something and she wasn't sure she could summon the strength to express the turmoil within her without making a fool of herself and confessing her need of him.

The sound of Thomas crying drifted down the stairs and they both turned in the direction of the sound.

'I'd better go and lift him,' Amanda said, standing up, thankful to slip away. With Thomas she could push the tragedy to one side and escape from the reality of the hurt for a while.

The following morning, Simon left for the airport. Jack tearfully begged him not to leave them, sobbing that he wouldn't come back. Having agreed to keep the children at home for the rest of the week, Amanda pacified him with a promise to take them down to the children's playground and they went as soon as Simon had driven away.

The sun was shining and a few young children were playing on the park. Before long, Jack and Rebecca had joined in the fun. Amanda envied their childhood ability to brush sadness away for a while.

The next three days passed by in a mist of unreality, punctured by sudden moments when reality intruded again. On her own with the children, the underlying sadness hung heavily on Amanda. She would be glad when Simon returned.

The sad news didn't take long to travel through the village and everyone was so kind. Pies, quiches and cakes appeared on their doorstep and cards of condolence came through the post.

Though she wouldn't admit it to anyone . . . hardly even to herself . . . Amanda missed Simon's presence. He was another adult to share the responsibility . . . and, suddenly, his space was vacant.

Until Saturday, Amanda hadn't been able to force herself to go into her dad and Kelly's bedroom, although she knew it would have to be faced one day. When the children were in bed, she went upstairs to check that they had gone to sleep. She looked at the closed door of the master bedroom. Maybe if she just stepped inside, she wouldn't find it too difficult?

Before she could change her mind, she pushed open the door and slowly advanced into the room, trailing her fingers along the chest of drawers. She crossed the room and glanced out of the window. The sky was still light and the sun shining just above the treetop to the right. It was a day to be alive . . . not . . .

She opened a wardrobe. It was her dad's. His suits hung there in neat rows; his shirts in the next one. They would need to be sorted and disposed of . . . but not yet.

Kelly's wardrobe filled a whole wall. There were dresses, trousers, suits, tops

. . . row upon row.

The dressing table top was littered with jars of cream, pots of make-up, lipsticks and perfumes. Her jewellery box was partly open; necklaces spilled out of it; rings and ear-rings sat in rows of velvet. These were Kelly's everyday jewels, and the costume jewellery looked cheap. As for the items which had once belonged to Amanda's mother, however, Kelly had insisted on being allowed to wear them.

'They aren't suitable for a child of thirteen!' she'd said to Doug when Amanda had protested. 'She'll get them back when she's older.'

Only she never had.

'What do you need good jewellery for? You don't go anywhere worth wearing them!' Kelly had said. 'You'll only lose them or give them away to your ever-grabbing friends!'

The more expensive items were stored in separate boxes. Some would be locked in the safe behind the picture on the wall. Others were probably in

Kelly's or her father's luggage, which was now on its way home.

Amanda sat on the edge of the bed and tipped the contents of the jewellery box on to the bedcover. She knew which were her pieces. Her mother used to let her wear them when she was watching her get dressed to go out with Dad. She used to put a ring on every finger, bracelets along the length of her arm and necklaces draped around her neck, one on top of the other. She would put a pair of high heels on her feet and pirouette around the room, feeling like a princess.

Finding comfort in the memories the pieces evoked, she began to sort them out. Those that had been her mum's she put to one side and those that were Kelly's she replaced in the box. She was unaware of time. Each item of her mother's had some special memory to linger over, to enjoy. A sapphire bracelet on her wrist; its matching necklace around her neck, she was fixing the second earring into her ear when

Simon's voice spoke behind her.

'What do you think you're doing?'

Amanda whirled round, her fingers still holding the earring in place. The coldness of his voice startled her.

'Simon! I didn't expect you tonight! I thought . . . '

'Obviously! So you felt free to rifle through my sister's jewellery box! She said you couldn't wait to get your hands on them! And now I see it with my own eyes! Were you intending to keep some of them? Did you think I wouldn't know?'

Amanda was aghast. 'No! That is . . . they're mine . . . Some of them, anyway. These . . . and these!'

'I've seen Kelly wearing those! And those others . . . and those! You disgust me! Couldn't you even wait until after the funeral before robbing my sister?'

Amanda's eyes blazed. 'Don't you dare accuse me of stealing! Your sister wore these pieces of jewellery because she took them from me!'

Simon scornfully raised an eyebrow.

'I don't believe you! Why would Kelly steal jewellery from you? She had plenty of her own.'

'Huh! You can say that again. She wasn't happy until she had a new piece of jewellery to wear . . . but not these! They're mine! They belonged to my mother and she left them to me when she died! There are plenty others for Rebecca. You can't really think I would take things that were rightly hers!'

'I don't know what you would be prepared to do, since you've hardly ever darkened the doorstep with your presence in the past few years!'

Amanda's cheeks reddened at the stab of truth. 'That wasn't by my choice!'

'Don't make out Kelly prevented you from coming!'

'We didn't exactly get on!'

'So she told me! I think you had better replace all the jewellery into Kelly's box until a full assessment can be made . . . by an independent assessor,' he added coldly.

Amanda stood up. The sapphire earrings were in her hand and she made no attempt to remove the necklace and bracelet.

'I make no claim on any of Kelly's jewellery!' she said quietly. 'My father gave them to her and that is that! But I'll fight tooth and nail for all that belonged to my mother!'

She looked steadily into his eyes, defying him to remove the sapphires by force. Her heart was thumping, knowing that if he made any physical move against her her shattered nerves would break and she would react hysterically out of control.

Thankfully, he didn't.

He stood aside as she stalked past him with as much dignity as she could muster.

6

An atmosphere of constraint hung over the next few days. Simon tried to convey a contrite air without actually apologising, since he wasn't totally convinced that he needed to. Kelly had complained enough to him about her troublesome step-daughter to fix in his mind the image of a self-centred, flighty, uncaring young woman who took every opportunity to thwart Kelly's attempts to befriend her.

He had to admit that Amanda's care of him whilst he had been under the effect of the viral infection had been commendable.

As for her handling of the children, he couldn't fault her dealings with Jack and Thomas but her impatience with Rebecca was often to be sensed lurking under the surface! All in all he felt uncharacteristically confused and busied himself with organising all the details of the double funeral, which was to be held as soon as all the formalities were through.

When the children were in bed, he shared with Amanda all that had happened in America.

'Do you mind if I go in to work for a few days?' he asked Amanda later. 'I need to talk over a few things with Nicola . . . and I also need to sort out some clothes. If you need to get in touch, I'll either be at work or in my apartment and I'll come back here at the weekend.'

Amanda didn't mind. He had his job to think of . . . and his relationship with Nicola. He couldn't be on compassionate leave for ever.

She also had her own future to think of and phoned the hotel to let them know of her changed circumstances. Rachel, one of her flatmates, telephoned immediately, saying how shocked they all were and that those not on duty at the hotel would come to the funeral.

'And don't forget to holler for help if you need any,' Rachel volunteered. 'I don't know what we can do but we'll do our best.'

Amanda was touched by her care and concern. Everyone who heard of the tragedy was so kind. Cards of condolence continued to arrive by every post.

At long last, the legal formalities were completed and both Amanda and Simon felt it a relief to be able to proceed with the funeral.

Doug and Kelly's bodies were to be flown on a Monday, and they fixed the funeral at ten-thirty on the Thursday. The church service would be followed by a buffet meal in the Church Hall, the catering to be provided by a local firm, and then the reading of the will would be at the house for just the family.

'Family?' she echoed in her mind. She had none now, except for her half-brothers and sister. Simon's father lived in London and she had overheard Simon talking to him on the telephone. She knew he would be coming for his daughter's funeral.

Simon's dad, Tony, was easy to get on with. On the whole, he hid his grief and used the occasion to get to know his grandchildren a little more. Jack and Rebecca loved him. He wasn't much older than Doug had been, so he was more of a father figure than grandfather to them. And Thomas was ready to take to anyone who would jump him up and down on their knee. He chortled with glee, flexing his chubby legs and springing high above Tony's head in his capable hands.

Simon, Amanda and Tony all agreed that the children should attend the funeral, since the service was going to be in the form of a celebration of Doug and Kelly's lives, remembering the good times and putting aside their grief for the time being.

Just before they were ready to set out, a low-slung red convertible swung into the drive and a long-legged blonde dressed in a top-of-the-range tailored suit, uncurled herself out of the driving seat. As she straightened her lithe body, she gazed appraisingly at the front of the house for a few moments before reaching into the open-top car for her slender clutch-bag.

Amanda knew straightaway that this must be Nicola . . . and she was right. Hmm, so Simon liked his women to be a picture of sophisticated elegance! Regretfully, she realised that she might as well opt out of contention now . . . because there was no way she could compete — not in any area . . . neither looks, nor career, nor the all-pervading confident manner that Nicole exuded as she approached the door.

Simon was still upstairs and so it was Amanda who went to welcome her, balancing Thomas in one arm as she opened the door. The two women appraised each other for a moment until Amanda remembered her manners and opened the door wider.

'You must be Nicola,' she greeted her. 'Do come in. I'm Amanda, by the way. Simon said you hoped to be able to come today. You're just in time to come to church with us. Would you like to wait in the lounge while I tell Simon you're here?'

'Thank you, Amanda. Oh, this poor motherless baby! What a tragic accident! I can't imagine what you're going through,' Nicola gushed as she stepped past Amanda. 'I know Simon was very fond of his sister . . . and those poor children, losing both parents like that! Whatever will become of them?'

'They still have me!' Amanda said more sharply than she meant to.

'And me!' Tony's voice spoke from behind Amanda. 'Nicola! Lovely to see you again! Thank you so much for coming!' Jack was with him, his face pale as he bravely held back his tears.

'Tony! You must be devastated!' Nicola stepped to meet him and they exchanged cheek-to-cheek greetings. 'I just had to come to be with you both. Suck a shock! And the children! The poor dears!' She patted Jack on his shoulder and then saw Simon coming down the stairs with Rebecca. 'Simon! How are you coping, dear? This must be so hard for you!'

She moved swiftly to the foot of the stairs and held up her face for him to kiss. 'And poor Rebecca! So sad!'

The doorbell rang again and Tony moved to open the door. 'It's the cortege,' he said quietly. 'Are we all ready?'

Nicola looked enquiringly at Simon. 'Surely, the children aren't coming to the funeral. Do you think that's wise?'

'They'll be better with us than here on their own,' Amanda said quietly. She felt a bit disembodied from the group. The other three adults obviously knew each other so much better than any of them knew her. 'We all need each other today.'

'Shall I take Thomas?' Simon offered, holding out his arms for him.

'No, I can manage,' Amanda assured him. 'He's almost asleep and it would be a shame to disturb him.' In reality, she knew she needed Thomas as much as, if not more than, he needed her. She leaned her head slightly, so that she was nestling her cheek against the baby's silken hair. He smelled comfortingly of baby soap and he contentedly snuggled into her neck on the short journey to the church along Higher Lane.

Amanda felt detached from everything as they followed the two coffins along the centre aisle to the front of the church. The words of the service were compassionate and comforting but it was as if it was all happening to someone else, with her as an almost invisible onlooker. Even when she saw some of her friends from the hotel in the congregation, it seemed as if they, too, belonged in a different world at a different time.

Thankfully, Simon shepherded them through the ordeal with a care that surprised even himself. Both he and Amanda had previously lost a mother and the memories of that time flooded back to merge with the new grief. It was with some relief that they eventually said farewell to the friends and colleagues who had attended the funeral and left the catering firm to clear everything away.

Amanda's flatmates and colleagues promised to be in touch in the near future. Their life together already seemed to be a whole lifetime away.

Back at home, Mrs Murphy had the kettle on and, although they had drunk more cups of tea than usual that day, it helped to have something in their hands as they awaited the arrival of Mr Smethurst, Doug's solicitor.

At exactly four o'clock, he rang the bell and was welcomed into the house. Thomas was having his afternoon sleep and Jack and Rebecca were playing under Mrs Murphy's supervision.

'You don't mind if Nicola sits in with us, do you?' Simon asked. 'As my partner, she's bound to be affected by some of the decisions that will have to be made.'

Amanda felt too numb to either agree or disagree, and so the four adults seated themselves at the dining table with Mr Smethurst. He put on his spectacles, gathered up the sheaves of paper and glanced around the table, making sure he had everyone's attention.

'I will be as informal as possible,' he told them, 'though, of necessity, some parts of the proceeding will be formal and couched in legal terminology. If there is anything anyone doesn't understand, feel free to ask for an explanation. Shall we begin?'

Everyone nodded and murmured their agreement.

'I have two wills here. This one is the Last Will and Testament of Douglas Purvey and this of his wife, Kelly Purvey. I must point out that I was responsible for only Mr Purvey's will being drawn up as I had taken six months leave of absence due to ill health when Mrs Purvey made out her final will. However, both began by naming the other as main beneficiary, which, sadly, is no longer applicable.'

Mr Smethurst looked up at this point and made eye-contact with each listener over the top of his spectacles.

'It seems that Douglas and Kelly were being attended by a different medical team. Both were unconscious when medical help arrived at the scene of the accident and neither regained consciousness at any time. On both of the death certificates, the time of death is written down as being at exactly the same time. So, you see the dilemma?'

'Which supersedes the other?' Tony murmured.

'Exactly!' Mr Smethurst agreed, glad to have appreciation of his problem.

'Does it greatly matter?' Simon asked cautiously.

Mr Smethurst regarded him approvingly. 'Only in two clauses, which I will come to eventually.' He cleared his throat and continued his informal explanation. 'However, when two people die at more or less the same time, as in this occurrence, it is customary to assume that the elder one died first, leaving the will of the other in the over-riding position.'

Amanda grimaced wryly. That meant Kelly's will would supersede her father's. Depending on the wording of her father's will, she could be left with nothing, for she was certain she didn't figure in Kelly's will!

'My task, as solicitor, and yours, Miss Amanda Purvey, as your father's executor and yours, Mr Simon Travers, as your sister's executor, is to try to determine what each testator had in mind when the wording was chosen,' Mr Smethurst continued, 'and how best to make sure that the intent of both parties is implemented without contravening the intent of the other. Are you with me?'

'I think so,' Amanda murmured, echoed by the others.

'Good. The problem will become clear when the particular clauses are laid alongside each other.' He cleared his throat again. 'I shall continue, starting with the Last Will and Testament of Douglas Purvey.'

After the opening preliminaries and the specific sums of money left to minor beneficiaries, Amanda found herself to be the first mentioned beneficiary.

'To my elder daughter Amanda Jane Purvey, I leave a fifth of my estate and any items of mine deemed to have belonged to, or been given to me by, her mother, my late first wife, Mrs Jane Purvey. Also, a fifth share in the house known as *The Laurels* or a fifth share of its eventual selling price. The house must not be sold except by full agreement of all beneficiaries or their representatives in the event of any being under the age of consent at the time. In the event that my wife, Kelly Purvey, predeceases me, I leave a quarter of my estate to my daughter, Amanda Purvey, and a quarter of the house value with the same proviso as above.'

Mr Smethurst resumed in his normal speaking voice. 'As you probably realise, this is one of the clauses that needs to be discussed. Do we agree?'

Amanda's brow furrowed. It seemed to be a question of whether she received a fifth or a quarter of her dad's estate. Kelly's fifth might be deemed to be added to her estate. She mentally shrugged. She could cope with that, she supposed. Everyone nodded and murmured agreement, content to let it rest for now.

'I leave the remainder of my estate to my wife, Kelly Purvey, and my three younger children, Jack Douglas Purvey, Rebecca Anne Purvey and Thomas Anthony Purvey.

'In the event of my wife, Kelly Purvey, predeceasing me, I nominate my daughter, Amanda Jane Purvey, to be the guardian of Jack Douglas Purvey, Rebecca Anne Purvey and Thomas Anthony Purvey in loco parentis until the above mentioned reach the age of twenty-one or their earlier marriage (under the trusteeship of my solicitor, Mr Geoffrey Smethurst or his official successor until Amanda either attains the age of twenty-five years or marries with their blessing).'

Amanda felt light-headed with relief. No-one could take her brothers and sister from her! They wouldn't be separated! She knew she was young at twenty years of age to be in charge of a six-year-old, a four-year-old and a one-year-old baby, but she could envisage no other possibility. Mr Smethurst would help and guide her and be on hand to advise on major decisions until she was twenty-five.

She felt her body relax, her relief evident upon her face. She vaguely wondered why Mr Smethurst didn't respond with any degree of enthusiasm to her delight but didn't dwell on his deficiency in that direction. After all, he had to display an impartial attitude to the proceedings, didn't he?

The reading progressed to Kelly's will. Apart from a nominal bequest to Simon, the bulk of Kelly's estate, if Doug had predeceased her, was to be divided between Jack, Rebecca and Thomas, which came as no surprise to anyone.

Amanda had put aside Mr Smethurst's initial warning of some conflict between the two wills until a change of tension among the three men alerted her to what was actually being said.

'In the event of my children, the aforesaid, Jack Douglas Purvey, Rebecca Anne Purvey and Thomas Anthony Purvey, being under age on my death, I nominate my brother, Simon Travers to be their guardian in loco parentis until they reach the age of twenty-one or their earlier marriage.'

7

Amanda sat bolt upright and exchanged a startled glance with Simon. She felt a cold hand seize hold of her heart, knowing immediately that he would challenge her for the right to be the guardian of her brothers and sister.

Simon seemed to be as startled as she was.

'Did you know about this?' Amanda asked sharply.

'No. I'm as surprised as you are.'

He turned to Mr Smethurst. 'So, what happens now?'

Mr Smethurst spread his hands. 'As I said earlier, we need to determine what was the intention behind each nomination and reach an agreeable conclusion to suit all parties . . . most of all, what is best for Jack, Rebecca and Thomas.'

'Well, that's obvious!' Amanda said quickly. 'They are my brothers and sister and I'm almost twenty-one. This is . . . was . . . my home. I will come back here to live and take care of them.'

'And if you wish to marry in, let us say, another year, what will you do then?' Mr Smethurst asked.

Amanda met his gaze unflinchingly. 'It would make no difference. I wouldn't want to marry anyone who didn't feel the same way about bringing up the children as our own.'

'And what about you, Mr Travers?' Smethurst asked, looking at Simon.

'I see no problem in me being the children's guardian. I have a good income, so there would be no problems there. Jack is at school and Rebecca goes to a nursery school until September when she, too, starts full-time education, I believe. And Thomas is due to start full-time nursery in September. I will work flexi-hours. I can't see any problems arising!'

'And what about in the evenings or if they're unwell?' Amanda snapped. 'You can't just put children in a box and open the lid when it's convenient!'

'I have noticed that phenomenon,' Simon agreed smoothly. 'I expect I could advertise for help . . . or even Dad, here. Many children are cared for by grandparents, I believe. What d'you think, Dad?'

Tony looked surprised. 'I'm duly flattered that you should think so . . . but I'm only fifty-three. I'm nowhere near ready to give up my full-time employment. I suppose I could try to get employment around here but it won't happen overnight. However, I'll give it a great deal of consideration,' he agreed. 'I've always said I never see enough of my grandchildren.'

Amanda opened and closed her mouth, aware of a sense of panic arising within her. 'And where does that leave my father's wishes?' she demanded. 'And my own feelings? Or, don't I count?'

'You will have as much access to them as you have now,' Simon said coolly.

'I want to give them more than that! They need me full time!'

'How will you manage to support the children as well as yourself?'

Amanda snapped her lips together and glared from Simon to Tony. She glanced at Nicola, whose face was a picture of shock. However, Nicola's reaction was Simon's problem, not hers!

'I would be prepared to make the children my full-time job, at least until they are all at school,' she declared passionately. She glanced at Mr Smethurst. 'I presume my father's estate will provide for the children's education and care.'

Mr Smethurst placed the tips of his fingers together and touched his chin with his forefingers. 'Ah! Now, that is another matter you will have to deal with.'

'What do you mean?'

Mr Smethurst pursed his lips. 'From the enquiries I have made to date in consultation with Mr Purvey's bank manager, it appears that some retrenching will have to be done in order to get things back on to an even keel. There seems to have been a great deal of expenditure over the past few years.'

Amanda bit back the scornful sound she had felt rise to her lips. No need to ask questions to discover the cause for that! Kelly was always demanding new things . . . clothes, perfumes, jewellery, cars and holidays.

She noticed that Simon and Tony exchanged wry glances.

'How bad is it?' Simon asked cautiously. 'This house? Is it secure?'

Amanda felt her heart lurch with anxiety when Mr Smethurst shook his head. 'Unfortunately, the house was remortgaged only three years ago. As you know, the repayments in the first few years cover little more than the interest and most of the mortgage is still outstanding. There are a few thousand pounds in the bank and various sound investments. Mr Purvey's bank manager, Peter Williams, will discuss this with you in greater detail.'

He looked over the tops of his spectacles at the anxious faces. 'Also, the immediate future needs careful handling. I'm afraid Mr Purvey was sailing very close to the wind and there is very little cash actually available at the moment. No, no! Don't look so alarmed! Mr Williams assures me that it can all be sorted with careful management . . . but he will need to see you as soon as possible. In the meantime, will you all think over your various options and phone my office when you are ready to see me again?'

He took off his spectacles with an air of finality and leaned back in his chair, sympathetic to the heavy silence that hung over his three clients.

After he had departed, Tony went to ask Mrs Murphy to make them a cup of tea and a plate of sandwiches. He touched Nicola on her shoulder as he passed by her and jerked his head towards the door, indicating that she follow him. With a show of reluctance, she did so, leaving Simon and Amanda looking at each other with a mixture of emotions visible in their demeanour.

Amanda felt angry at the worry Kelly had caused her father. She thought back to the day her father had met her at the railway station. She had sensed then that something was amiss.

Simon looked at her with a modicum of sympathy. In his opinion, Doug had been too weak in handling his monetary affairs . . . too anxious to please Kelly; too afraid of losing her. However, he knew that he and Amanda had many decisions to make and, if they were to have any hope of working in harmony, he had to make a move right now. He leaned forward.

'I understand how you're feeling Amanda,' he began gently.

'Do you?' she responded coldly. 'You haven't shown much understanding so far this afternoon!'

'I was as startled as you were by the two wills. I'd no idea what Kelly had in mind. She should have asked my opinion.'

'There are a lot of things Kelly should or shouldn't have done!'

Simon inclined his head in partial agreement. 'Did your father tell you of his nomination of you as the children's guardian?' he asked quietly.

Amanda was stumped. 'Well, no . . . but he knew I would want to look after them.'

'As Kelly knew I would. Look, Amanda, we've got to work together in this. I know Kelly had many faults but she was my sister. Mum died when she was twelve and she went wild. I spent the next ten years picking up the pieces. But that's in the past now.'

He paused and looked straight into Amanda's eyes. 'Let's not make the same mistakes again. We can work it out together.'

Amanda raised her eyes to meet his. She knew she wouldn't always agree with him . . . and would let him know it! But they both had the good of the children at heart.

She nodded slowly. 'We . . . and your dad . . . are all the family they've got.

I'll play my part.'

Tony decided to stay on for a few days before going home to Sussex. He thoroughly enjoyed helping with the children and it gave Amanda some time to relax and his presence eased the awkwardness between her and Simon.

'Keep in close touch with me,' he said before he left on the Sunday morning. 'I'll consider moving up here if it means I can be of any help.'

He looked steadily at the two of them. 'The main burden rests on you two. Think carefully before you make a final decision . . . and listen to each other.' He smiled ruefully at them. 'I can't help noticing you both seem to leap at each other's throat without much thought. Whatever your preconceived ideas about each other, leave them aside. This is now . . . and the children's future. Don't mess it up!'

Simon and Amanda exchanged glances, both unwilling to bend . . . but acknowledging the truth of what Tony was saying.

'You'll bear my words in mind?'

The question was directed at both of them and both nodded, warily eyeing the other.

'Good . . . and, as I said, keep me informed.'

Nicola came for lunch. Amanda didn't actively dislike her. It was just that she knew she wasn't really interested in the children. She barely spoke to them and when she did, it was in a stilted manner. She just wasn't family oriented . . . an opinion confirmed just before Nicola left after a noisy family tea-time.

Amanda was in the process of putting Thomas in his cot but, due to the fact that he was cutting a tooth, he was a little bit grizzly and she was rocking him to sleep in her arms, crooning softly to him, when she heard Nicola's voice right outside the room.

'I think you're crazy to want to take on three children, Simon! You realise it will ruin your career, don't you?'

'I don't see why,' he protested. 'I'm

sure Amanda will stay on and help.'

Nicola's next words make her hackles rise. 'Huh! Well, you know what she's after! The lion's share of your inheritance!'

'It isn't my inheritance . . . it's the children's. But, I'm against Amanda being the one to get control. She hasn't got the necessary experience, however much she'd like to persuade Mr Smethurst that she has.'

Amanda knew she ought to step out on to the landing and let them know that their conversation was being overheard but Thomas had just fallen asleep and she was reluctant to risk waking him.

'Go and talk it out somewhere else!' she silently directed through the door.

Her plea went unheeded. 'Well, you'd better watch out or you'll find yourself playing 'Mummy and Daddy' for real!' Nicola scorned.

'Don't be ridiculous, Nicola! That's the last thing I'm thinking about! I hardly know the girl!'

'Well, don't expect any support from me on this, Simon! Let Amanda have them! They're her brothers and sister, after all!'

'Kelly entrusted them to me. I won't let her down!'

'I'm beginning to think your sister's death has taken the edge off your sense of judgment,' Nicola told him coolly. 'That's it, then! You're on your own!'

'That's the way I work best, Nicola! The one out front on his own!'

'Except this time I think you'll be the one left behind! So long, 'partner'! I'll see you at the office!'

Amanda stood stunned by the overheard conversation with a mixture of emotions running through her. Anger at Simon's swift rejection of her as a possible girlfriend . . . 'the last one he'd choose,' she reminisced ruefully . . . and equal anger at Nicola's casual disregard for the children's welfare and her equally casual rejection of Simon. Knowing Simon would be embarrassed to know she had overheard the conversation, she laid Thomas in his cot and waited until all was quiet outside before she went downstairs.

They were both quiet that evening. They bathed the children, enjoying the splashing and bath time fun and both read them a story and listened to Jack and Rebecca's bedtime prayers.

The little girl was sitting in bed with her hands folded and her eyes closed. 'Please God, look after Mummy and Daddy and give them a kiss from me and Jack and Thomas.'

As on every previous night, the simplicity of her prayer brought a lump to Amanda's throat . . . and a swift glance at Simon's face showed that he was similarly affected.

As Amanda was about to rise and drop a kiss on her cheek, Rebecca continued, 'And don't take Amanda and Uncle Simon away from us. Amen.'

Amanda glanced once more at Simon, wondering what Rebecca had overheard, aware, of course, that Simon didn't know what she'd overheard. Well, she'd forget about that for now. The main thing was to reassure Rebecca that she wasn't about to be abandoned.

'He won't, darling. We're here to stay.'

Simon raised an eyebrow, looking mildly concerned. Amanda made a wry expression as she rose and helped Rebecca to snuggle down under the light duvet, kissing her cheek.

Simon had to return to work on Monday, but he arranged to take Wednesday afternoon off in order to see Peter Williams, the bank manager.

They spoke with Mr Williams in the dining room. The picture he gave was much as Mr Smethurst had said. Cash flow was falling to a low level but, with prompt action, the situation could be lifted out of danger. He steadily eyed them in turn.

'Let's start with this house. I'm afraid it will have to be sold.'

'Is there no other way?' Amanda asked desperately. She had spent her childhood here. Her mother had lived here. It was where she always thought of as home, even after her father had married Kelly.

Mr Williams shook his head. 'It's a large house with high running costs — council tax, heating, lighting, general upkeep, the gardens, and domestic help. On top of that, the mortgage is too much for you to repay. Even when your father's business is sold, there won't be enough to cover it and provide running costs for the future.' He looked at Simon. 'I haven't yet asked you how you stand financially, Mr Travers, but you would have an extremely exceptional salary if you were able to cover the monthly repayments.'

Simon shook his head. He knew that he didn't, not without putting his business at risk.

Over the next two hours, Mr Williams led them through his meticulously worked-out figures, leading to the indisputable fact that the only way to clear the debt and leave enough money to give Jack, Rebecca and

Thomas a secure future was to sell all the present assets and use part of the resultant money to buy a less prestigious house with a more modest mortgage agreement.

After a short discussion they decided to sell both the Spanish apartment and the cottage in Cornwall at the end of the season, after honouring all lettings. Both the BMW and Kelly's soft-top convertible went straight onto the *for sale* list. A smaller family car wouldn't cost a great deal and would be more practical, especially when put alongside Simon's Honda.

An informal assessment of individual pieces of Kelly's jewellery suggested that at least fifty thousand pounds could be raised after Amanda, Jack, Rebecca and Thomas had chosen, or had chosen on their behalf, an item to have as a keepsake.

'I've got my mother's jewellery,' Amanda said, with a sidelong glance at Simon, who narrowed his eyes slightly and raised his right eyebrow as if surprised by her audacity. Unrepentant, she continued, 'I don't mind the pieces being valued and will relinquish anything that I have to in order to settle all of this . . . but I'd like to choose my piece from amongst those.'

Mr Williams nodded. 'That's fine by me. Maybe if you sort it out and submit it separately, we'll see what the valuer comes up with.'

And Kelly's selection of designer clothes were to be sent to a shop in Manchester that had a retail outlet for second-hand high-class fashion items.

'There is still the debt from the lifestyle Mr and Mrs Purvey were accustomed to . . . domestic help and lavish entertaining,' Mr Williams continued. 'Mr and Mrs Purvey were living on an overdraft. Even with a smaller house, you'll have to budget carefully. Are you up to it, I wonder?'

'I've been managing my own affairs since I was eighteen,' Amanda informed him. 'I'm sure I could learn to manage on a larger scale. I presume you would help me in the early stages, Mr Williams.'

'Of course. What about you, Mr Travers?'

'I don't foresee any problems in that respect,' Simon answered unhesitatingly, carefully avoiding catching Amanda's eyes, knowing she would regard it as a stab in the back. 'I did my training in accountancy and run my own business successfully.'

Amanda's mouth dropped open. She hadn't realised Simon ran his own business. She'd thought he was employed like many other young men of his age. It made her aware that there was a lot about Simon she didn't know. He wasn't one who liked to talk about himself and she had never felt able to pry.

'Now, the only remaining question is, what is your commitment to Jack, Rebecca and Thomas? You're both young, Mr Travers and Miss Purvey. You can't pick up a child and put it down again two years later.'

'I'm committed a hundred per cent!' Amanda said swiftly.

'And the same for me!' Simon urged.

Mr Williams nodded. 'I admire your sense of obligation . . . both of you. Have you considered what would happen when either of you want to marry? You're likely to, you know. What if your prospective partners didn't feel the same level of commitment?'

'Then I wouldn't marry!'

Again, it was Amanda who spoke first, but Simon was swift to echo her words, their eyes meeting briefly.

'And how do you foresee the handling of the day-to-day matters?' Mr Williams looked over his spectacles at Amanda. 'Maintaining a cash flow and taking care of three young children?'

'I'm sure I'd manage,' she retorted firmly, in spite of her reservations. 'Better than you!' she glared at Simon. 'Rebecca and Thomas start school and nursery in September anyway. I'd be able to get a job then.'

Simon glared back. 'I would hire someone with my own money.'

Mr Williams carefully replaced the cap on his pen and slipped it into his top pocket before he responded mildly. 'No-one expects any binding statements at this early date. You're here with the children now, giving them the love and stability they need. Don't hesitate to get in touch with me if any problems arise. In the meantime, I'll get the ball rolling for the various valuations and I'll telephone you to arrange date and time, etc. The sooner we get the house on the market, the better.'

After he had gone, Amanda flopped forlornly onto the sofa in the lounge but forced herself to put on a bright air when Simon entered the room. It wouldn't do to let him think she was ready to throw in the towel, even though, at this very moment, she felt she was staring defeat in the face.

Simon sat on one of the chairs. When Amanda looked at him, she saw that he too was looking pensive.

'Penny for them,' Simon said.

Amanda gave a laugh. 'I don't think they're worth a penny!'

Simon shrugged. 'Let's face it. It's a

tough one, isn't it?'

Encouraged by his attitude, Amanda decided to be honest with him. 'The fact is, I have to accept that I can't manage on my own. I could probably manage all the physical aspects . . . but, unless Mr Williams' figures are over pessimistic, I won't have enough money.'

'And I possibly just about earn enough money . . . but that doesn't leave any time to see the practical part.' He gave her a lop-sided smile. 'You wouldn't consider my earlier suggestion of being the paid help, would you? That would solve most of the problems. I'd be able to work and you'd have the care of the children.'

Amanda wondered how serious he was. On the surface it sounded an easy way out of their problems . . . but she wasn't going to give up that easily!

'I don't like the idea of being paid to look after my own brothers and sister,' she objected. 'And where would you be living? It wouldn't be very satisfactory for you to live in your flat and be just paying out on all the bills.'

'I know I'm in a good position financially, but I'm still building up my business and I couldn't afford to run two places. I'd have to live here. Would that be a problem to you?'

Amanda shrugged. She didn't mind in principle but she wasn't sure how she would cope with him bringing girlfriends home. Even if Nicola kept to her threat of leaving him, there were bound to be others. She liked him a lot more than she cared to let him know and, apart from his occasional lack of regard for her, he didn't seem to dislike her . . . apart from when Kelly's misrepresentations of her made him think otherwise and, surely, he must see that she wasn't as bad as Kelly had painted her? But would that make them ideal home-mates?

'I'm not sure,' she began hesitantly. 'People would talk. Would it reflect on the children? And what if I wanted to bring a boyfriend home? Wouldn't it seem a bit strange?'

'Have you got someone in mind?'

'No, but you never know. Or you might want to bring a girlfriend here. And, if it got serious, would that mean the other one would have to move out? I can't see it working out really. Can you?'

'There is another alternative.'

'And what's that?' Amanda asked sharply, wondering if he was going to suggest once more that she bowed out of the situation.

'We could get married.'

8

Simon was as surprised as Amanda appeared to be. The words had slipped out before he could stop them. Looking at their effects on Amanda, it didn't seem to be one of his better ideas!

'Are you serious?' Amanda demanded, a note of incredulity in her voice. It was only a week since Nicola had broken their relationship! Talk about 'off with the old and on with the new'!

'It was just an idea,' he apologised, deciding to back down before he got in too deep. 'I suppose I wasn't really thinking.'

That wasn't quite true. He had been thinking about it ever since Mr Smethurst had spoken to them but hadn't got as far as making a definite decision. His long-held opinion of Amanda had been undergoing a tumultuous change since she had come into his life so suddenly . . . but had he moved on so far as to be in love with her? They had both been hurtled into this situation and it probably wasn't the best of times to be making such a long-term commitment. On the other hand, long-term commitment was exactly what the children needed.

Amanda appeared quite aghast at his suggestion. 'Well, if that's the way it was, I don't think much of it!' she exclaimed. 'Honestly, Simon. I can't believe you're joking about this! We've got very realistic problems and we're going to need realistic answers! Not something that flits across your mind and you speak it out without thought!'

Her face flushed and Simon felt he had upset her. Not wanting to make things worse, he held up both hands, palms towards her.

'Just a thought! Just a thought! Obviously not a good one! We'll just have to let the neighbours think we're living in sin and show them we don't care!'

'Well, I care!'

She wasn't a prude and knew a number of people who were living together without taking the step of being married . . . but that wasn't for her! She couldn't understand where Simon was coming from. It seemed only yesterday that he was mistrusting every word she spoke and losing no opportunity to tell her so. And now he was proposing marriage . . . but admitted he hadn't given it much thought!

In spite of her lingering youthful adoration of him, she wasn't keen to enter into such an arrangement without her feelings being shared. Which left them exactly where they were with a bagful of problems and absolutely no answers.

'So, what do you suggest?' Simon asked coolly.

'I don't know!' Amanda snapped, his suggestion of marriage having knocked her emotions sideways.

'Well, we have to come up with something before very long, so don't spend too much time thinking about it!'

The sound of Thomas crying drifted down the stairs and Amanda was thankful of the excuse to break-up the argument before it became too heated or too personal.

'Thomas seems to be waking up. I'll have to go and change his nappy. He's teething and is showing signs of a nappy rash.' She paused in the doorway and looked back to Simon. 'What are you doing for the rest of the afternoon?'

'I'd better go back to work for a few hours. I've got a lot of catching up to do and I need to see Nicola about something.' He looked uncomfortable. 'Do you mind if I stay in Manchester until Friday evening? I need an early start in the morning.'

Amanda wasn't sure how true that was. He was probably anxious to get away from her spontaneous rejection of his ill-timed proposal.

'That's fine!' she said brightly. 'And maybe you'll have a word with Mrs Murphy before you go, and tell her we're putting the house up for sale.' Amanda knew she would miss her. She had grown used to relying on her sound commonsense approach to rearing small children. But, she was an expense they couldn't afford!

During the night, Thomas's endless crying reinforced her anxiety about the situation. She lost count of the number of times she had to go into the nursery to comfort him. In the end, she decided to take Thomas into her own bed. She wasn't totally sure it was a good thing to do but it seemed to be the only way she would get any sleep that night.

The next day, after taking Jack to school, Amanda took the other two children to the park, wondering if this was to be the pattern of her life from now on. Had she been too hasty in turning down Simon's unexpected proposal? Maybe they could have made it work?

As they passed the parish church she saw a notice saying that a Mother and Baby Club was taking place there that afternoon. At least she might meet others in a similar situation there and after a hasty lunch, Amanda returned with the children. It was good to watch Rebecca playing with other children and Thomas playing nicely with the other babies.

Amanda had chance to chat to some of the young mothers. Some assumed that she too was a mum and let it ride, not wanting to explain the intricacies of the situation. There were a couple of girls she remembered from school and enjoyed catching up on local news and gossip. All-in-all, it was an enjoyable afternoon and Thomas fell asleep in his stroller on the way to pick Jack up from school. That gave Amanda time to concentrate on the two older ones and she played a board game with them before making their evening meal of fish fingers and oven chips.

'I like mayonnaise with chips,' Rebecca told Amanda. 'Mummy let's me put my own on.' Her face crumpled as soon as the words were spoken. 'I mean . . . '

Her eyes brimmed with tears and she hung her head. 'I'm sorry,' she muttered. 'I forgot. I haven't got a mummy any more, have I? Who's going to look after us when you go back to work like Uncle Simon? Will it be Mrs Murphy?'

'I've got to look after you,' Jack said quietly. 'Daddy always said I'm the 'man of the house' when he's away . . . only I don't know how to do it. What's going to happen to us, Amanda?'

Amanda drew them close and hugged them. 'Uncle Simon and I will look after you,' she said determinedly, pushing aside the problems that entailed.

'Can you and Uncle Simon be our mummy and daddy?' Rebecca asked.

Amanda's heart seemed to spasm. 'Is that what you'd like?'

'Yes, and I could be your bridesmaid and wear a long dress.'

'And I'll even dress up as a page boy,' Jack offered gallantly, 'though I'd feel a bit soppy!'

Amanda's heart contracted. What could she say? She thought of Simon's proposal again, wondering again if she should have accepted it. She truly didn't know. And now it seemed that he was intending to try to persuade Nicola to think again about being willing to take on the children. She hugged the children.

'Unfortunately, it's not that simple, but don't worry. We'll both take care of you for as long as you need us.'

During another sleepless night, as Amanda paced the floor with a tearful Thomas in her arms, she had more than enough time to think about the problem — but her thoughts weren't exactly coherent. The screams of the teething baby seemed to drive every sensible thought out of her head and out of the open window.

Jack and Rebecca's boisterous behaviour the following day tested her patience to its limit and she was ready to throw in the towel when Simon returned home looking more relaxed that she felt.

'Hi, kids! I've brought you some

treats!' he greeted them, tossing a bag of assorted chocolate snacks to them, which Rebecca and Jack pounced upon with glee.

'Not until after tea!' Amanda said sharply, looking crossly at Simon.

The children moaned but accepting the ruling, sorted out the packets between them.

Simon picked up Amanda's irritation. 'How's it been?' he asked conciliatorily. 'Have you had much time to relax?'

'No, I haven't!' she snapped. 'And I've only just got tea in the oven!'

Over dinner, she poured out her woes, partly ashamed of her grumpiness but unable to restrain herself. Simon probably had no idea what looking after three children entailed! At least he took over the children's bath time, which gave her time to tidy up downstairs, but he then spent the evening going over some of the reports on his laptop computer.

'I'm having an early night,' Amanda finally announced, having learned from the previous two nights that it was best to sleep whilst Thomas slept in order to cope when he woke up.

When Thomas did awaken, it seemed to Amanda that she had only just fallen asleep. She groaned and peered at her bedside clock. It was 1.23 am.

Thomas was standing miserably in his cot, his cheeks bright red and tears streaming down his cheeks. He refused the sip of cool water Amanda offered him in his drinking cup, knocking it out of Amanda's flailing arms.

'Poor baby! It's hurting, isn't it,' Amanda soothed. She got out the teething gel and smeared some of it on to Thomas's inflamed gums and jogged him up and down for a few minutes. After a few minutes, it seemed as though he was settling and Amanda gently laid him back into his cot and tiptoed back to bed.

No sooner had she settled down, than the crying started again. She lay for a few minutes, hoping Thomas would go back to sleep. But he didn't.

Where was Simon? How come he didn't hear any of this?

She sighed and dragged herself into the nursery. She went through the same procedure as before, changing Thomas's nappy in case it was that that was upsetting him, but it didn't seem to be wet.

This time, Thomas settled for over an hour. Amanda had gone straight back to sleep and so it seemed to be only a few minutes since she had staggered back to bed when the ear-piercing screams penetrated her mind. It was 3.19 am.

She lay on her back, her eyes screwed tightly shut as she murmured, 'Go back to sleep, Thomas!' When he didn't, she distractedly ran her hand through her tousled hair. She couldn't cope with this on her own!

In desperation, she stalked into the nursery, picked up Thomas from the cot, took his drinking cup and the tube of teething gel off the cupboard and marched into Simon's room.

'Wake up! It's your turn!' she declared, putting Thomas on to the bed and shaking Simon's shoulder.

Simon groaned and turned his head to the other side. 'Wake up, Simon! Thomas needs you!'

Simon rolled over again, slowly rousing from his deep sleep. Thomas began to cry. At such close quarters there was no escape. Simon's eyes flew open in alarm.

'What's the matter? What's wrong with him?'

'He's teething and won't stop crying! I've had two nights of this already and I'm at the end of my tether! I can't stop him crying and I don't know what else to do!'

To her embarrassment and consternation, she burst into tears. She thrust Thomas into Simon's arms and sank down on to the bed, her head in her hands.

'Hey! Come on, now! It's not that bad! Is it?' Simon asked, pulling himself out from under the bedcovers and kneeling on the bed at Amanda's side. He held Thomas in one arm and put the other around Amanda's shoulders.

'It's like you said, he's teething. It'll pass. See, he's quiet now.'

And, indeed, he was, as if his nocturnal adventure into Simon's room had spontaneously driven away the pain.

For a moment, it seemed to Amanda as though everything was going to be all right and she leaned her head against his shoulder. His voice held so much care, she suddenly felt confident that her love for Simon that had been a part of her life for the past seven years and had blossomed into more than a fantasy in the past week or so, was now being returned. She had been too hasty in turning down his unexpected proposal!

Simon's face was very close. She could feel his breath fanning against her cheek and she gave in to her intense longing to turn her head slightly. Their lips were almost touching and she didn't know if it was herself who had drawn nearer or Simon . . . or maybe both had moved at the same time?

The kiss was exquisite. Tremors of delight rippled through her body such as she had never known before. Thomas let out another wail of distress, breaking the bond that held them captive to each other. Their bodies separated and, although Amanda couldn't see Simon's face clearly, she could hear his ragged breathing and knew that it matched her own.

'Hmm, saved by the yell!' Simon quipped lightly. He had pulled slightly away from her but his hand still rested on her shoulder and she could still feel his warm breath on her face.

'Yes.' Amanda's voice was no more than a whisper. That kiss had blown her mind away! What was he thinking? She felt confused. Was he falling in love with her, after all? Was the break with Nicola a permanent one? Had she been a bit hasty in turning down his proposal? Maybe she should have thought about it first? Or at least talked it over with Simon?

Perhaps it wasn't too late to do so! It was what Jack and Rebecca wanted! And, if she were totally honest, so did she! Her heart raced excitedly and she leaned towards him again. With unerring judgement, their lips met. It was all Amanda had dreamed about for seven years. She felt she was melting inside.

'Simon?'

'Mmm?'

'Er, about your proposal the other day? I've changed my mind. My answer's yes!'

His body stiffened. 'What?'

She smiled in the semi-gloom. 'I've changed my mind . . . yes, I'll marry you!'

He jerked away so suddenly that Thomas, who had stopped crying, was jolted back to wakefulness and let out another yell. Simon automatically jogged the arm that was holding him. 'Come off it, Amanda! You were right the first time! Marriage without love wouldn't work! It wouldn't be fair to the children! They've suffered enough!'

Amanda's heart sank. He wasn't even

prepared to give it a try!

'We might fall in love,' she tried desperately, knowing that for her, she already had.

Simon laughed harshly. 'Even people who start off in love often drift apart, regardless of whether there are children or not. Starting off with children who aren't even ours would make it worse, not better. And it would have to be for life! We couldn't marry and then split up. It would destroy them!'

'Well, then, we'd better come up with a different plan now that we've given that one a good airing!' she said with false brightness as she stood abruptly to her feet, reaching down to take Thomas out of Simon's arms. 'It's a good thing one of us stayed in control of our faculties!'

The baby was nearly asleep again and Amanda prayed he would remain so.

'I'll pace the floor some more until he settles again. Sorry to have spoiled your sleep! I'll see you in the morning!'

With hot tears burning her eyes, she

took Thomas back to the nursery, gently placed him into his cot and then slipped hastily back to her room. A soothing hot drink would have been good but she was afraid to go down to the kitchen in case Simon had the same idea.

Once in the safety of her own bed she lay on her back staring up at the ceiling, allowing the tears to flow freely down her cheeks and neck and soak their way into her pillow. One thing was clear. Whatever they decided to do, she had to get over her infatuation with Simon . . . and try to convince him that she felt no more for him than he did for her.

Sleep didn't come easily. The problem of the children's need for care and the best way to provide it, churned over and over in her mind. What could they do? She wanted to be the one to look after them but she couldn't do it on her own. She didn't have enough money, not if she had to pay off the mortgage of whatever smaller house they found.

Maybe she could persuade Simon to contribute monetarily without actually living with them? Would that make her a 'kept woman'? She almost giggled at the old-fashioned word. But would it be fair to expect Simon to stay at a distance if he was providing the money? He had a genuine love for his young nephews and niece.

She froze at the thought that he might win custody of them if it came to a court case. She couldn't bear it. They were her brothers and sister. She loved them. They belonged together. The thought of some unknown women looking after them paralysed her mind.

It came back to him paying her. Did she want to be beholden to Simon for keeping them together? The answer was simple. No, she didn't! But it would be better than losing them altogether.

The sky was almost light when Amanda's eyes finally closed, her problem unresolved.

Consequently, it was very late when she awakened. When she reached the kitchen, Simon was already breakfasting with Rebecca.

'You're late, Amanda!' Rebecca accused. 'Uncle Simon made my breakfast!'

Amanda glanced at Rebecca's almost empty bowl of cornflakes. 'That was clever of him!' she said tartly, riled by Rebecca's naïve praises of Simon's efforts. 'Maybe he'll make your lunch as well . . . and your dinner!' It was a low hit, she knew, but, as she hadn't many weapons to use, she had to use all that she had.

Rebecca looked at Simon expectantly. 'Will you?' she asked. 'Can I have chicken nuggets and chips and lots of ice-cream?'

Simon raised a querying eyebrow in Amanda's direction, correctly interpreting her attempt at sarcasm. 'Sorry, Rebecca. I'd love to make your lunch, but I'll be at work. I'd better get my skates on!'

Jack looked full of admiration. 'Golly! Are you really going to skate to work, Uncle Simon?'

'I might!' he grinned. 'Some people do!' He rose from the table, ruffled Jack's hair and dropped a kiss on top of Rebecca's head. 'See you later, kids.'

Amanda sensed his glance fall upon her but she busied herself getting the bottle of milk out of the fridge, dreading that he would see the naked longing in her eyes for a similar token of affection as that given to her sister.

She had to stop loving him! She had to! But it wasn't that easy. How could she, when that strange little butterfly movement in her stomach reminded her of it every time she thought of him!

The house went up for sale. People came to view; people came to indulge their curiosity. It was a lovely house, set in beautiful gardens. It didn't need anyone to sell it — it sold itself. A firm offer had been received by the end of the second day.

Amanda was shell-shocked. Selling her home was something that was going to happen at some indefinite point in the future — not today! To make matters worse, the buyers wanted the completion date as soon as possible.

'It can't be done!' Amanda wailed, needing more time to get used to the idea of losing her home.

'They've agreed to the full asking price — as long as everything goes through without hold-up,' Simon pointed out mildly. 'Accept the fact that we can't keep it! It's only brick and mortar for heaven's sake!'

Amanda couldn't so easily turn her back on her home. 'It's more than that. It's memories . . . my childhood, Mum, Dad . . . everything! I've got nothing left!'

'You've got . . . '

To his consternation, he almost said, 'You've got me!' What was he thinking? They'd already gone through this and he didn't want to go through it again.

' . . . the children,' he added lamely.

Amanda looked at him steadily. 'Have I?' she asked quietly. 'What if you get custody of them?'

Simon knew where her fears and

anxiety were coming from. He moved closer and put his hands on her shoulders. Amanda met his eyes. He could see the helpless sadness and grief in them . . . and concern for the future. Once again he felt a wave of compassion flow over him, swiftly followed by an urge to offer protection. He managed to stifle the impulse.

Instead, he said, 'We'll work something out, Amanda. Somewhere we could all live near together but separately . . . I don't know . . . like an apartment or something.'

Amanda frowned. 'I'm not sure I'd like the children to live in an apartment. They need a garden to play in but . . . ' She paused, as an idea sprung into her mind. 'How about something that has a 'granny flat'?' she suggested. 'There are some houses on 'Parklands' like that, but I think they are restricted to people over the age of fifty-five. There'll be others, though. You often see them advertised.'

The new idea put life into the

situation and over the next few days they eagerly scanned the local papers and estate office advertisements. Their need was noted and promises of early notification given. However, it was Simon who found the ideal place. He arrived home one evening waving a sheaf of papers in his hand.

'This might be just what we're after,' he said, opening the folder and displaying a new housing estate that was in the process of being built. 'The only trouble is, it's not round here. It's on the outskirts of Bolton. It's right on the edge of the countryside, like here, but in easy reach of town. A railway runs close by, with a direct line to Manchester, so I could come home every night without having to drive through city traffic. It sounds ideal. What do you think?'

Amanda nodded. 'Let's go and look at it, and take it from there.'

They went on Saturday. The building site was well under way, although none with a granny flat was completely finished yet. Some houses had already been taken but a number were still available. Of these, there were only two with an attached flat and one of those was the show house.

They had three bedrooms; a spacious living-room; a dining-room that overlooked a reasonably sized garden; a kitchen large enough for a family to eat informal meals in it; and a good-sized bathroom. The granny flat had one bedroom; a bathroom, a small living-room; and a small kitchen, all on the ground floor. It also had its own separate front door.

'What do you think?' Simon asked Amanda when they were in the show house.

Amanda slowly turned around, drinking in all aspects, wanting to be sure in her mind before she spoke. A slow smile spread across her face.

'It's ideal! Can we afford it?'

Simon nodded. 'I've already had a word with Peter Williams. He's worked out a reasonable mortgage repayment.'

Amanda's smile hid her inner apprehension. Could she cope with living in such close proximity to Simon without betraying her love for him? If that was the only way to keep the family together, she would have to! She pushed her thoughts aside and took a step towards the door.

'Come on, then! There's only two of this style left. If we ask for this show house, we'll be able to move in as soon as the other one is sold. Let's get our names down before someone else grabs it!'

They drove back to Rainford in high spirits. Suddenly, they seemed to have turned a corner, with everything beginning to go their way. They had only been hone ten minutes when the phone rang. Amanda couldn't hear all that Simon was saying, but she could tell from the tone of his voice that the news wasn't good.

'What is it?' she asked, when he returned to the living room.

'A slight set back. The show house

has already been taken. The other plot won't be available until the end of August.'

'Oh.' Amanda felt deep disappointment. 'What did you tell them?'

'I said we'd talk about it. It doesn't mean we can't have it. We'll just have to put the furniture we're keeping into storage and rent something for a few weeks. We might even be able to squeeze into my apartment for a few weeks.'

Amanda hadn't seen his apartment but Simon had already told her it only had one bedroom and a small boxroom.

'I'm not sure,' she said doubtfully. 'What would the children do all day in the middle of a city?'

'Have you got a better idea?'

'Not at the moment, but I'm sure I will!'

'Shall I ring back and confirm our agreement, then?'

'Yes. I don't think we'll find anything more suitable!'

Her optimism was rewarded. The phone rang mid-afternoon. The caller introduced himself.

‘Hello. I’m John Rowlinson. Can I speak to Mr or Mrs Purvey, please?’

Amanda’s heart contracted. Would it never get any easier? ‘I’m sorry. Neither of them is available. There was an accident. They . . . they died. I’m Doug’s daughter.’

‘Oh, I’m sorry. I don’t want to cause any distress to you. It’s just that I’ve rented their cottage in Cornwall for the summer but an unexpected family crisis means we need to return home at the end of next week. We won’t be able to come back here before our lease runs out, which means the cottage will be vacant for the remainder of the season.’

Amanda’s heart leapt within her. ‘Yes. Thank you,’ she answered. ‘I appreciate your thoughtfulness.’

Inside her head, she was leaping with joy. That’s what they’d do! The school holidays were due to start next week. She’d take the children to Cornwall and give them the sort of holiday she’d had as a child.

9

The next two weeks passed in a whirl of activity. Amanda sorted through every cupboard and every wardrobe, packing clothes to take on holiday, and sorting through everything else. The storage firm would see to the household items . . . kitchen utensils, ornaments, crockery, bed linen and so on. She merely whisked through everything to sort out obvious charity shop items.

The activity left her exhausted by the end of each day but she was glad to be kept busy, and it gave her the excuse to go to bed early, instead of spending cosy evenings with Simon. He didn't make any objections and she presumed it suited him as much as it did her.

With her route planned and the car packed, it was hard to believe that it was the last time she would walk out of her childhood home. Jack and Rebecca were excited and Simon full of last-minute instructions and suggestions of when to stop for a break and which roads to avoid.

It was late when they arrived at the cottage. It had been a long, tiring journey and the children were fast asleep. Amanda got out of the car and stretched her body, turning her neck slowly from side to side. She breathed in the cool night air. Mmm! She remembered the scent! It was a mixture of honeysuckle and the salty air. Her weariness evaporated and she unlocked the door of the cottage.

Mr Rowlinson and his family had left the place beautifully clean. She quietly unlocked the boot of the car and got out the bag with their bed linen, hoping the children wouldn't awaken until she had made their beds.

They didn't . . . and she soon had them settled in bed. Thomas hadn't wakened at all and Jack and Rebecca had only stirred long enough to sleepily ask if they were there.

Simon moodily drifted about his apartment. What was the matter with him? He couldn't remember experiencing this aimless restlessness before. It wasn't something he enjoyed. It was only as he lay sleepless in his bed that he acknowledged the truth. He was missing his newly acquired family, and they had only been gone a few hours — but he didn't know what to do about it.

The call of the seagulls awakened Amanda. It was only 6:30 in the morning but she felt fully awake. She slid out of bed and padded across the bedroom to draw back the curtains. The cottage stood on the top of the cliffs of West Pentire, overlooking the wave-swept sands of Crantock beach to her right and rugged cliffs to the left. A sense of satisfied exhilaration flooded through her body and she breathed in deeply, drawing into her being not only the salty fresh air but also the nostalgic peace and beauty of the place.

She had been right to come here. Her

memories of the holidays she had spent here with her parents would help to mellow the pain of her father's death — and, hopefully, help to erase the different pain of her unrequited love of Simon. Only when that healing had been accomplished could she move into the future. However difficult that might be, she would do it. She had to! The children needed her.

The first couple of days passed quickly. Simon telephoned to make sure they had arrived safely and Amanda was pleased with how distant she had managed to appear in the tone of her voice and, afterwards, convinced herself that the sound of Simon's voice hadn't affected her in any way at all.

The weather was glorious and they followed the same daily routine. A hurried breakfast . . . no need to chivvy the children to get on with it; clear away the breakfast dishes and do a hasty tidying up; pack all Thomas's requirements into a large beach-bag; and make sure the other two had all of their essential items, such as buckets and spades and Rebecca's back-pack of doll and doll's clothes.

She bundled Thomas into the push-chair, locked the door and headed for the narrow path that wended its way down the cliffs to the sandy beach below. Jack and Rebecca skipped ahead. Amanda was pleased at how well they had settled in the relaxed and simple lifestyle of their holiday existence.

They talked of their mummy and daddy at bedtimes but, with childhood acceptance, were no longer deeply distressed. They often asked if Simon was coming to stay with them and Amanda tried to be noncommittal in her reply, hoping that they weren't missing his male-presence too much.

The tide was full during the mornings, only turning around noon, which suited their present routine. It made a smaller area of sand for Jack and Rebecca to wander in, yet provided ample sand for digging and building sand castles. They would have qualified for digging a whole market garden, Amanda decided, watching their effort — a hole nearly all the way to Australia and a castle worthy of its name . . . or would have been if Thomas didn't keep throwing himself on to it, chortling with delight.

'Thomas!' Jack remonstrated. 'Amanda! He's done it again!'

'Never mind. He's only a baby.'

'You've got your hands full, there!' a masculine voice observed.

'Pardon?'

Amanda swung around, finding a tall young man with short spiky blond hair grinning down at her. She had noticed him surfing yesterday but there weren't any big waves at the moment. She smiled back.

'Yes. I could do with another pair of eyes and hands,' she admitted ruefully, wishing, not for the first time, that Simon were with them. She was missing him more than she had thought and it wasn't getting any easier. 'I'd no idea of how energetic they can be! To me, sand is strictly for sunbathing on, not digging for victory!'

'Summer job, is it? Are you a student?'

'No, to both,' she laughed. 'They're my brothers and sister . . . well, half-brothers and -sister. They're my full-time job!'

She knew her voice had saddened. 'For now, at least,' she added, injecting some life and vigour into her voice. She didn't want to talk about their family tragedy, not here within earshot of the children, nor to a stranger.

'Are you a student?' she asked without giving the young man any time to follow up her statement with any probing questions.

'Yes. Third-year medic. Rick Burgess is the name. I'm working with one of the pleasure fishing boats but we've closed for lunch. Mind if I join you? I usually try to get in some surfing but the sea is too flat today.'

'I'm Amanda Purvey and these three are Jack, Rebecca and Thomas. I saw you surfing yesterday,' she remarked as Rick settled comfortably on the sand at her side, instantly wishing she hadn't said anything about noticing him. 'That is, it could have been you . . . or someone else. It looked great.'

'It is! You'll have to give it a try! Maybe you could leave the kids with someone and come and see if you like it?'

Amanda shook her head regretfully. 'I'm sorry, it's not possible.' She didn't want to say they were there on their own, not to someone she had only just met. 'No, Thomas! Put it down!' she called out, seeing a shell about to go into the baby's mouth. She leaped up, glad to have a diversion.

Rick stood up too and went to give Jack and Rebecca a hand with their digging. Thomas toddled over to join in the fun and soon the five of them were busy digging and demolishing amidst cheerful laughter.

'I wish Uncle Simon was here,' Rebecca said suddenly.

'You've got me instead!' Rick laughed. 'Won't I do?'

'I s'pose so, but it would be nice if Uncle Simon could come!'

'Is he your favourite uncle?'

'He's my only uncle! He helps Amanda to look after us.'

'Uncle Simon is working!' Amanda said firmly.

'Oh! Am I treading on his preserve?' Rick asked casually, turning to face Amanda.

'N . . . No! Of course not!' Amanda replied quickly. 'He's the children's other guardian, that's all!'

'Well, that's all right, then. Just as long as I'm not in danger of being thumped on my nose!'

Rebecca burst into a fit of giggles. 'Uncle Simon wouldn't do that! Would he, Amanda?'

'I shouldn't think so!'

They chatted easily for half on hour or so until Rick noticed that it was time to go. 'Maybe I'll see you tomorrow?' Rick said on leaving.

Amanda shrugged casually. She didn't really want to form a holiday friendship, but didn't want to appear churlish. 'We're generally down here in the mornings,' she said pleasantly.

'And we're going to look in the rock-pools when the tide has gone out,' Jack informed him. 'We might find a crab!'

'You'd better save it for me to see!' Rick laughed. 'So long, then!'

His departure made Amanda feel more lonely than ever. Getting Simon out of her system was harder than she had anticipated it would be. The fact that he telephoned each evening didn't help matters. The sound of his voice still had the power to turn her insides to jelly, though she struggled hard not to let it show in her replies.

Rebecca kept begging him to come to see them and on Thursday evening, when he phoned, he said that he was finishing early on Friday and he hoped it would be all right for him to motor down there for the weekend.

Amanda's heart flipped . . . then commonsense prevailed and she reminded herself that he had no romantic notions about her and his presence would only stir up her own barely suppressed emotions.

'It's a long way,' she said in as matter-of-fact tones as she could manage.

'That's OK. I like driving.'

Her heart flipped . . . then came down to earth as he added, 'I miss the children.'

His frank admission put her mind into a spin. Did that mean he wanted to claim total custody of them after all? No, surely their joint arrangement would work out all right?

'Is that Uncle Simon?' Jack's voice interrupted her thoughts.

'Er, yes.'

'Goody!' He grabbed the phone out of Amanda's hand. 'It's lovely here, Uncle Simon, but we miss you! When are you coming?'

Amanda could hear his reply. 'Tomorrow,' he said.

'That's good. You can help Rick build a sandcastle and come out in his boat with us.'

'Who's Rick?'

'Amanda's friend. He's nice, but we like you the best!'

Amanda heard him pause before replying. When he did, his voice was quite normal. 'Good! Make sure you keep it that way!'

Amanda hardly slept that night. First she would find herself longing to see Simon again, then dreading the same. She imagined a heart-stopping reunion, followed by a cool disregard of her tumultuous feelings. How could he care when she did her best to keep her feelings for him hidden?

Then Jack's mention of Rick being her friend made her blush and then pale. What must he think of her? She had only been down here a week and already had an admirer.

Her churning mind suddenly stopped. That was her answer! Rick would be her protector . . . a proof that her heart wasn't broken by Simon's rejection of her — and Simon could make of it what he would!

Jack and Rebecca wanted to wait up to see Simon on Friday but Amanda wouldn't hear of it.

Her feelings of panic about once more sharing a dwelling place with him made her wonder if she had made a mistake in agreeing to share the house at Lostock on the outskirts of Bolton. If the thought of two days together was doing this to her, how could she possibly cope with the more permanent arrangement?

It was no use. She would have to see Mr Smethurst and convince him that it would be better if she were to have the sole guardianship of the children. She tried to push away the niggling thought that it would only be better for her! Simon wouldn't agree that it was better for him . . . and neither would Jack and Rebecca!

No, she would have to get over all this nonsense! Why, oh, why, did he have to decide to come down to Cornwall so soon? If only he had left her to lick her wounds a while longer, she'd have got over him!

Who are you kidding, she berated herself as she made the sofa into a bed and laid out a sleeping bag and pillow. She'd never get over him! And wasn't even sure she wanted to. What she needed to do was to learn how not to let her feelings for him show. Treat him cool! Keep her feelings under wraps! And, on that hopeful note, she checked that the key was in its hiding place . . . and went to bed.

'Good morning, campers!' Simon's voice rang out cheerfully.

Amanda groaned and pulled the duvet back over her head.

'Wake up, Amanda! Uncle Simon's here!' Rebecca cried excitedly, jumping on to the bed and hauling back the duvet.

'Go away! I'm still asleep!'

'No, you're not!' Jack joined in. 'Uncle Simon's got your breakfast ready for you! You've got to sit up!'

Amanda opened one eye. Her hair was tousled and she looked sleepily delightful. Simon was surprised by the lurch of his stomach. He held out the tray.

'Wakey-wakey! Rise and shine! I've only got two days with you so we have to make the most of them!'

It didn't take them long to have breakfast and tidy the cottage. Thomas caught the children's excitement and bounced up and down, hanging on to Simon's leg.

'Da-da-da!' he chortled.

'No, he's not!' Rebecca corrected. 'He's Uncle Simon!'

'He can't say that,' Simon explained. 'It doesn't matter for now.'

'I wish you could be my daddy . . . and Amanda my mummy,' Rebecca said wistfully. 'Everyone at nursery school has a mummy and daddy, except for me.'

Simon briefly met Amanda's eyes, noticing that she swiftly looked away.

He wished he could read her mind. How much did she care for him? Was there a chance that it could be deeper than her teenage crush? He wished he could think so. He noticed her heightened colour. Was that a positive or negative reaction? Maybe there would be an opportunity to talk about it during the weekend?

They had a busy morning on the beach. The children were as brown as berries and well-protected by sun-cream.

'When are we going in Rick's boat?' Jack asked.

'After lunch.'

Simon felt a pang of jealousy. Was Amanda already attracted to this new guy?

Later, they made their way down to the jetty, wearing their wind-proof jackets, in case it was chilly out at sea. Rick welcomed them aboard and showed them where to park Thomas's push-chair.

Simon eyed Rick, trying to convince

himself that he felt no jealousy about his free and easy manner with Amanda.

He scowled even more when he saw Rick sit beside Amanda with his arm casually resting across her shoulders along the boat's rail, and Amanda's bright smile churned his stomach. Did she genuinely care for him? Had he realised too late that his feelings for her went deeper than he had supposed?

When they reached the fishing area, Rick was busy helping other passengers and Simon seized the opportunity to put the bait on to Amanda's line and show her how to cast it into the sea. Then he did the same for Jack and Rebecca, holding the line with them and feeling ridiculously pleased when they got a bite.

On the way back, Rick pointed out some caves, telling the passengers that they were thought to have been used by smugglers long ago. Jack listened avidly to all that he said.

'What did they hide in there?' he asked, his eyes wide.

'Barrels of rum and pieces of eight!'

'What's that?'

'Golden coins! Lots of money and other treasures!'

'Are they still there?'

'You never know! They might be!'

That night, Jack demanded a smuggler's story before they went to bed and Simon invented a story about two children who found a smuggler's cave and dug in the sandy floor and found a chest of gold. They drank in every word, especially as the children in the story had their names.

'Do you mind if I go out with Rick?' Amanda asked him when the children were settled in bed.

He did mind — but could hardly say so! Especially since Amanda had been tied in every night with the children.

'No, that's OK,' he said lightly. 'I'll read or do a crossword.'

He couldn't settle to either. What a mess he'd made of everything! He should have seized his moment when Amanda suggested they get married!

Except, he hadn't been aware of his changed feelings. He'd thought it too risky. Maybe it still was? He shouldn't have come down here. He should have waited until they were settled in their new house. His mind filled with a sense of hopelessness, he decided it might be best if he left earlier on Sunday than he had originally meant to and he pretended to be asleep on the sofa-bed when Amanda returned, preferring not to hear about her scintillating time with Rick.

10

Amanda didn't really enjoy her evening out with Rick. She had accepted his arm around her shoulders when she thought it might make Simon jealous or make him think she no longer had any thoughts about there being any romance between the two of them, but when no such pretence was needed, she found herself disinclined to respond to Rick's amorous overtures. It didn't take Rick long to take the hint and Amanda was glad to make an excuse to go home to the children, thankful that she had driven into Newquay in her own car.

Not looking forward to facing Simon too early, she parked her car overlooking the bay and watched the sun sink down into the sea. It seemed to represent her hopes of Simon ever falling in love with her and she felt overwhelmed by a sense of extreme sadness. She couldn't help wishing that Simon hadn't come down to the cottage.

The darkening sky stirred her awareness of the late hour. She sighed and turned the ignition key, determined not to let Simon detect her sad mood.

Letting herself into the cottage, the sound of Simon's regular breathing from the sofa bed made her feel perversely annoyed and it was only her innate consideration for others that prevented her from going into the kitchen and making herself a mug of hot chocolate. When she finally fell asleep, it was to restless dreaming and, in the morning, her head was far from clear.

'Too much to drink?' Simon enquired.

'What if I did?' she snapped back. 'It was my first evening out since . . . since . . . '

In spite of her resolve to put on a cheerful front, her voice faltered and she was aware that tears weren't far away. She turned away and busied herself getting a jug of milk out of the fridge. It was still hard to accept that her dad and Kelly were never coming back. Would it ever get any easier?

Simon instantly felt a rush of compassion. He reached out and touched her shoulder. 'I'm sorry,' he said quietly. 'You seem to be coping so well, I forget how hard it must be for you.'

Amanda longed to turn towards him and bury her face against his shoulder but she was afraid that if she let the tears start, she wouldn't be able to stop them . . . and Rebecca was already looking at her with a worried frown on her face.

'I'm fine!' she said, brushing his hand away. 'Just a bit tired, that's all.'

By lunchtime, Simon decided that he might as well start on his return journey to Manchester. He had hoped to be able to have a heart-to-heart talk with Amanda but it was obvious to him that she felt uneasy in his presence. He knew it could signify a whole range of feelings but he wasn't eager to discover that there was no hope of a relationship between them.

'I'll set off as soon as we've had lunch,' he said quietly, as they returned to the cottage from a children's playground they had found.

'OK,' Amanda agreed, lifting Thomas out of the pushchair and setting him on to his feet. 'Keep an eye on the children while I get it ready.'

'You said you'd take me to see the smuggler's cave!' Jack protested.

'Next time,' Simon assured him lightly, ruffling the top of his head. 'The tide's coming in soon. We wouldn't have time to get there and back.'

'We wanted to go today!'

'Forget it, Jack!' Amanda said sharply. 'Simon is going and that's that!'

'Don't shout at him! It's not his fault we can't get on!'

'Oh? And I suppose you think it's mine?'

'I didn't say so!'

'You don't need to!'

'Oh, for heaven's sake! Don't bother

with lunch! I'm going now!'

Simon strode into the cottage, flung his few belongings into his bag and tossed it on to the back seat of his car.

He stooped down to hug the children.

'Don't go, Uncle Simon!' Rebecca pleaded tearfully.

'I have to. I've got to go to work tomorrow.'

'Stay until tea-time!' Jack pleaded.

Simon glanced at Amanda but saw only bleakness in her eyes. He shook his head.

'Sorry, kids. It's best I go now.'

'When are you coming back?'

He gently tousled Rebecca's hair. 'I don't know, soon, I expect.'

He looked back at Amanda. 'Bye, then. I'll be in touch.'

Amanda felt near to tears. She didn't want him to go like this, but didn't know how to stop him.

'Yes,' she said briefly and picked up Thomas, mainly so that she could avoid looking directly at Simon, hoping he wouldn't realise how upset she felt.

Simon got in his car and started the engine. With a brief smile at the children and a wave of his hand, he set off. Rebecca let out a cry and set off down the road after him. Through his rear mirror, he saw Amanda place Thomas down and run after Rebecca.

She caught up with her and restrained her, holding on to her arm as she struggled to free herself . . . and his car swung round the corner out of sight.

'You sent him away!' Rebecca sobbed.

'No, I didn't. You heard him, he has to go to work!'

'Was it my fault he went?' Jack asked. 'Did I make him cross?'

'No!' Amanda assured him. 'He had to go sometime today. He'll come back, maybe next weekend.'

'I don't want him to have to keep going away! I want him to stay with us! I wish he could!'

Amanda sighed. 'So do I, love . . . but he can't! Now, you'll have to play nicely together whilst I make some lunch. I'll put Thomas back in his pushchair so that he can watch you.'

It didn't take her long to make a few sandwiches. They could eat them out on the grass like a picnic. Feeling more cheerful herself, she carried the sandwiches and plates outside on a tray. 'Jack! Rebecca! Lunch is ready!'

Where were they? It wasn't like them to stray away. She ran round the back but there was no sign of them.

'Jack! Rebecca! Where are you? Come here at once!'

She was beginning to feel alarmed. They had been upset about Simon leaving. Had they set off to follow him? She ran back to the front and looked anxiously down the road. It was only about two hundred yards to the corner. She looked hesitantly back at Thomas in the pushchair, undecided whether or not to leave him there while she ran as far as the corner.

Thomas was bouncing up and down in the pushchair. 'Becca! Becca!'

Amanda stopped and stared at him

carefully. Was he saying his baby version of Rebecca's name? If so, considering that he was looking intently along the cliff top, was that where he had seen Jack and Rebecca go? Going by her gut instinct, she grabbed hold of the pushchair handles and set off along the narrow cliff top path. Once she had crested the rise she could see quite a long way . . . and there, bobbing about in the long grasses and cliff top flowers, were Jack and Rebecca's bright red T-shirts about five hundred yards ahead!

'Jack! Rebecca!'

Motivated by a mixture of anger and apprehension, Amanda resumed the chase, moving as swiftly as she could with the hindrance of the small wheels of the pushchair. There was no fence to guard the cliff top and although the path was set back a few yards, there was no guarantee that the children would stick to the path, even though that safety measure had been impressed upon them when they had strolled along there together.

'Jack! Rebecca!'

She was gradually gaining on them and, this time Jack heard her and turned round. Not far beyond them, the cliffs took a sharp curve inland, making it necessary to veer to the left with the path. Amanda was afraid that the children might keep on the straight line. She guessed they were trekking along the cliff tops to where the caves would be.

'Wait for me, children! I'm not cross with you! We'll go together!'

Rebecca turned away and began to run.

'Rebecca!' Amanda shouted again. 'Stop her, Jack!'

She abandoned the pushchair on the path and began to run over the grass in the shortest line. She saw Rebecca hesitate and begin to turn when she felt the ground beneath her feet began to slide away beneath her and she felt herself falling downwards into the ground. She flung out her arms to try to stop herself but the tall grasses that she grasped hold of were rooted too shallowly to take her weight and they barely checked her downward slide.

It was happening so fast that she was only aware of falling down an uneven, rocky 'chimney'. The angle of the 'chimney' had flung her on to her side and she managed to twist over slightly so that she was on her front, frantically grabbing at the rocky surface as she bumped down it. In her terror, she barely felt the pain of the grazed skin on her legs, abdomen and arms and a sudden downward drop removed even that poor contact.

The jar of landing feet first shot through her for a mere second before she crumpled on to a hard surface and collapsed into a heap, swallowed by pain and then a merciful blackness.

Simon drove for the mile or so into Crantock village feeling desperately unhappy. Men didn't cry! But he felt like doing so! He pulled over to the verge and switched off the engine. It was no use! He couldn't leave it like this! He would have to go back!

He gave himself a couple of minutes to calm his thoughts. He would tell Amanda of his changed feelings towards her and beg her to give them a chance to develop a loving relationship. He knew she used to have fond feelings for him . . . he remembered his embarrassment at her dogged *puppy-love*. He shouldn't have rushed her with his initial proposal, nor rejected hers so callously. Neither should he have let Kelly's jaundiced view of Amanda colour his own perception of her.

He grimaced ruefully. Regardless of his affection for his sister, he knew she had never been a *woman's woman!* She didn't like others of her own sex and always sought to pull them down and undermine them. He had taken too long to admit his error . . . and now he had to pave the way to reconciliation!

Ten minutes must have elapsed since he had driven away but he was surprised that there was no sign of Amanda and the children. He frowned at the sight of the dropped plate of sandwiches on the grass and stared around.

Where were they?

They couldn't have been gone long, since Amanda had had to make the sandwiches. They couldn't have gone down the road, or surely he would have seen them, and Amanda knew the tide was coming in so she wouldn't have taken them down the cliff path to the beach. They might be on the rocks though.

He ran to the cliff edge and looked down towards Crantock. No sign of them there. What about Vugga Cove to his left? He ran along the cliff top to the steep path down to the rocks overlooking the cove, her favourite spot, Amanda had told him, for diving and swimming when she was younger. But no sign there, either and it looked far too dangerous for small children anyway, he decided.

So where? The cliff top to his left seemed the only option. He hurried up the rest of the slope and shaded his eyes against the sun to enable him to see more sharply the figures in the distance. It was them!

As he took his first step towards them he heard Amanda shout Rebecca's name, followed by a scream and Amanda disappeared from view!

Had she slipped? Or worse, fallen over the cliff? His heart beating rapidly, he raced along the path, shouting, 'Stay where you are, Jack and Rebecca!'

He glanced down at Thomas when he reached the pushchair but the little boy didn't seem too distressed and so he raced on through the long grasses, regardless of any danger to himself. He was expecting to reach the edge of the cliff where he supposed Amanda had slipped over and was appalled to suddenly see the gaping hole in the ground almost under his feet.

He halted abruptly and then dropped to his knees and crawled forward to peer over the edge, instantly realising what had happened. Jack and Rebecca were running towards him, the scared look on their faces mingled with relief at his return.

'Stay back!' he warned, holding out his hand, palm forwards.

'Uncle Simon! Amanda's gone! She just disappeared!'

He didn't want to frighten them. He got to his feet and gathered them into his arms, hugging them tightly. 'I think Amanda has slipped down the cliff a short way,' praying that it was so! 'Now, I need you to be good children and go and stand by Thomas's pushchair. Don't move away from it until I tell you. You've got to look after him whilst I see what I can do here.'

Rebecca's mouth trembled. 'Is it my fault Amanda's gone? I ran away from her. I didn't mean her to fall.'

'We wanted to see the caves,' Jack admitted tearfully. 'Amanda said we'd to wait until after lunch, but we came when she wasn't looking.'

'It's not your fault, kids. It's just one of those things that happen from time to time. Now, go and look after Thomas.'

Jack and Rebecca reluctantly left him and Simon dropped down on to the grass again and peered down into the darkness.

'Amanda!' he called. 'Can you hear me? It's Simon!'

He listened intently but couldn't hear anything. Was she still alive? He felt threatened by an overwhelming sense of panic that he sought to quench. He wasn't sure he could cope if she were dead, not on top of everything else. If he hadn't been sure before about how much she had come to mean to him, he was now! He couldn't bear to lose her.

'Amanda!' he called again, his voice high with fear. 'Are you there? Please answer me! I love you!'

He could feel his heart pounding against the rocky ground under him and, for a moment, forced all his muscles to relax. Keep cool and think!

He knew Amanda must be down there. She couldn't be anywhere else, but following her down into the unknown would hardly help the situation.

He glanced over his shoulder. Jack and Rebecca were clutching the handle of the pushchair, their wide, frightened eyes fixed on him. He forced the semblance of a smile.

'Stay there, I'm going to phone for help.'

He fumbled in his trouser pocket for his mobile phone and quickly stabbed at 999. It was answered promptly.

'Hello! My name is Simon Travers. I'm on the cliff top at West Pentire and my . . . my girlfriend has fallen down a hole in the cliff . . . no, I can't see her . . . nor hear her . . . I don't know how deeply she has fallen. Another problem, I have three young children with me . . . Pardon? Oh, about five minutes ago . . . hang on, I'll try again.'

He put his head directly over the ragged opening and listened intently. He could hear the sound of lapping water, but nothing else.

'Amanda!' he called loudly. 'It's Simon. Can you hear me?'

He strained his ears and thought he caught a faint sound.

'Try again, Amanda! I love you!'

This time he was sure he heard her.

'Are you hurt?'

'A bit.' Her voice was faint but he was sure of the words. He felt a surge of relief.

'Can you see anything?'

Her words were indistinct but he caught, ' . . . dark. Wait . . . bit of light!'

'From up here?'

' . . . below.'

Simon repeated all he had heard to the emergency operator.

'Ask her if she can move.'

He did so, and waited for Amanda to reply.

'Not sure! . . . ledge . . . hear water.'

He could hear the panic in her voice. 'Is the ledge wet or dry?'

'Not sure . . . cold.'

'OK, you're doing fine. I've called for

help and the coastguards are on their way. Would it be safe for me to slither down to you?'

There was a pause, then, ' . . . need ropes . . . drop!'

It seemed an eternity before he heard the powerful engines of the coastal rescue boat but it was probably less than five minutes. They circled around far below but didn't approach the cliffs. Why didn't they get in there? She must be in some sort of a cave, mustn't she? Couldn't they send a small boat in? The sudden dread of the opening being too small hit him. Too small for a boat or a swimmer — but large enough to let the rising tide in!

One of the men in the boat was gesturing up to the sky. Simon followed the line of his gesture and wondered that he hadn't heard the noise of the rotor blades. Jack and Rebecca were pointing up, too.

'Stand absolutely still!' he called, not daring to move from where he was in case he couldn't find the crevice again among the grasses. 'They're coming to get Amanda!'

The helicopter landed and three men jumped out, hauling with them a huge folded metal contraption, which they swiftly assembled over the hole, revealing it to be a tripod frame that soon held a motorised winch. After a quick conversation with Simon, the slenderest man of the rescue team was helped into the harness.

'Call down to your wife and tell her we're on the way,' he said to Simon, as the harness was secured. 'Tell her to keep as close to the wall as she can and to make conversation as soon as she is aware that I'm getting near. What did you say her name is?'

'Amanda.'

'Right, Amanda! I'm coming down!'

Down in the depths of the cliff, Amanda waited in growing anxiety. She could tell by the sound of the water that the tide was rising within the underground chamber and she had no way of knowing whether or not she was above the high water mark. Now that her eyes had grown used to the dark, she could make out the dim forms of her rocky prison but, as her rescuer began his descent, most of the light was blocked out by his body and she realised that the rising tide was blocking it out from the lower end.

At least the sounds of rescue brought some comfort . . . and the memory of Simon's words. Did he really mean it, that he loved her? Or was he just saying it to comfort her and give her a reason to hang on?

Some loose stones rattled down the chimney space above her, announcing her rescuer's progress and almost immediately, he began to speak to her.

'Hello, Amanda! My name's Bob. Am I getting near to you?'

'I can hear you more clearly than I could hear Simon. You can't be far away.' She remembered the sudden drop at the end of her fall. 'Watch out for a drop at any time. It felt like ten feet or more, I'm not sure.'

'Don't worry. I'm hooked on to a safety line. Shield your face if you can, then my feet won't swing into you.'

The time seemed endless. She was sure that she could feel water lapping at her feet and hoped she'd be able to stand or in some way assist Bob to get her up to the surface again. Her ankle hurt and her hands were sore. She didn't dare try to stand on her own in case she fell and made her situation worse.

The last few minutes passed quickly. Bob was suddenly crouching on the ledge beside her and she felt his arms reaching for her. She clutched at him and found herself sobbing against him. He patted her back reassuringly.

'You're going to be all right, Amanda. Let's get this bodyboard under you and this harness around you. You'll go up in front of me. And don't worry, I'll be alongside you most of the time. I'll call instructions up to those strong hunks above us. We'll have you out in no time at all.'

It took a bit longer than that, but, inch-by-inch, she was gradually pulled to the surface. The sudden light made her eyes blink but, when she opened them again, the first face she saw was Simon's. She tried to reach out to touch him but her arms were fastened to her side.

Simon recognised her intended gesture and gently touched her cheek. She knew she was crying but couldn't stop herself.

'You came back,' she whispered.

'I realised I had to tell you I've grown to love you . . . and risk you telling me there was no chance. Could you learn to love me again, do you think?'

Amanda managed to blink away her tears and smile. 'I never stopped loving you, silly! But, what about Nicola? Didn't you make up with her?'

'Nicola? What's she got to do with it?'

'You said she was your partner . . . only I know she didn't want to have the children.'

Simon's brow creased, as he tried to

make sense of what Amanda was saying. A vague memory struggled to surface. 'She's my business partner. I've never been in love with her.'

'Oh!'

Jack and Rebecca came running over the grass. Rebecca stood with her hands on her hips.

'Does this mean you'll be our mummy and daddy, Amanda and Uncle Simon?'

Simon and Amanda exchanged glances and read the agreement in the other's eyes.

'It seems so,' they both answered.

'That's good,' Rebecca declared. 'So, can I wear a pink dress and have flowers in my hair. Why are you all laughing?'

'You'll never have a dull moment, mate!' one of the men laughed.

'Thank goodness for that!' Simon smiled.

Books by Karen Abbott
in the Linford Romance Library:

RED ROSE GIRL
SUMMER ISLAND
A TIME TO FORGIVE
LOVE IS BLIND
LOVE CONQUERS ALL
A MATTER OF TRUST
DESIGNS FOR LOVE
WHEN TRUE LOVE WINS
A TASTE OF HAPPINESS
THE HEART KNOWS NO BOUNDS
THE TURNING TIDE
OUTRAGEOUS DECEPTION
RISING TO THE CALL
A FRENCH MASQUERADE
A HEART DIVIDED
DANGER COMES CALLING
TO FACE THE PAST
DANGEROUS INTRIGUE
JUST A SUMMER ROMANCE
AN UNSUITABLE ALLIANCE
HER RELUCTANT HEART
AFRAID TO LOVE
TO CAPTURE A HEART

FAITH FOR THE FUTURE
A CHANGE OF HEART
ILLUSIONS OF LOVE

We do hope that you have enjoyed reading this large print book.

Did you know that all of our titles are available for purchase?

We publish a wide range of high quality large print books including:
Romances, Mysteries, Classics
General Fiction
Non Fiction and Westerns

Special interest titles available in large print are:
The Little Oxford Dictionary
Music Book, Song Book
Hymn Book, Service Book

Also available from us courtesy of Oxford University Press:
Young Readers' Dictionary (large print edition)
Young Readers' Thesaurus (large print edition)

For further information or a free brochure, please contact us at:

Ulverscroft Large Print Books Ltd.,
The Green, Bradgate Road, Anstey,
Leicester, LE7 7FU, England.
Tel: (00 44) **0116 236 4325**
Fax: (00 44) **0116 234 0205**